NUMBER ONE FAN

SAMANTHA GAIL

DSTAR PUBLISHING LLC

For my mother, Kelly. Thank you for always humoring me in my obsessions.

ONE

"Dolian Crawford is set to become the world's highest grossing actor of all time at just 29 years old."
-*People Magazine*

Imogen Reilly did not have time for the security guard to question her press badge. Did it look a little manhandled after her brother, Austin, played with it? Absolutely. But that certainly didn't mean the guard had the right to deny her access to the press box at the red carpet premiere of Dolian Crawford's latest movie.

This was the kind of opportunity most journalists and celebrity bloggers salivated over. It was her chance to finally get up close and personal with the entertainment industry, which was exactly the kind of break she needed. Her weekly blog, *Hollywood Unmasked*, hadn't exactly "unmasked" anything yet.

The homunculus guard standing in front of her now,

blocking her entry, with his black sunglasses, bulging biceps, and angry scowl prevented her from doing just that.

"Sir, is there any update?" Imogen asked him. The first security officer took her badge into some unknown "computer area" to look up her credentials and left the man-troll behind to scan in press badges as journalists and preferred paparazzi arrived.

The man's face was immovable as he turned her way before rotating back to the next guest.

Imogen already felt completely out of place because of her clothes. She had never been to a movie premiere before and assumed she needed to dress as though she herself belonged in Hollywood rather than as the broke reporter living in a tiny, five floor walk up in Compton with her mother and adult brother with Down Syndrome that she was. Everyone else who walked up so far appeared more casual and muted, wearing comfortable shoes, solid colors, and the same over-caffeinated, harried look.

People tended to write her off because she looked so much younger than her 22 years, with a waif-like figure and far below average height. Her soft brown eyes and tawny hair were unremarkable. And thanks to her nonexistent budget, Imogen shopped in the juniors' clearance section more often than not. A great choice when you're trying to stretch a dollar into five. An unforgivable choice when you're trying to blend in with the Hollywood elite as a celebrity gossip blogger.

That was why she wore the only dress she owned that made her look old enough to attend a red carpet premiere without a chaperone. However, a Barbie pink vinyl mini-dress purchased for a dollar at a dead hippie's garage sale in the Valley made her look far more appropriate on Hollywood Boulevard than anywhere else. Add that to her only decent pair of heels, large white platforms that made her tall enough to reach the top shelf at the grocery store, and Imogen stuck out like a sore thumb. She tried to pair it with diamond (aka cubic zirconia) hoops and silver bangle bracelets up both arms, but neither did much to soften the harshness of her appearance.

More than one entering press member sent her a scathing look of annoyance.

Finally, the first guard who took her badge returned. "She's good," he said incredulously to his partner.

"Thank you!" Imogen sang out, snatching the badge from his outstretched hand and shuffling as fast as she could down the makeshift hallway leading to the press box.

TWO

"Dolian Crawford as Agent Ruthless *is a force to be reckoned with.
Is there any role this man can't best?"*
-Leslie Hughes, Oprah Magazine

Everyone around her looked bored and irritated to be there, and Imogen couldn't imagine why. Attending the world premiere of Dolian Crawford's latest blockbuster, *Agent Ruthless,* was the most exciting thing to ever happen to her. Not only could this be her big break, a chance to actually report on something that brought real readers to her blog, but it was the first time she would ever see Dolian in person.

While the average teenager outgrew their first celebrity crush, Imogen had yet to do so. Dolian Crawford had adorned her walls since her freshman year of high school when his breakthrough role as the hunky heartthrob in the teen flick, *Passions,* put him on her radar. Thankfully for her, his perfectly sculpted six pack, twinkling blue eyes, and dimples put him on everybody's radar. His career took off like a rocket, landing him on every magazine cover known to man. Every film became a box office hit with Dolian's name attached, and he made Hollywood history when he became the youngest actor ever to win back to back Oscars.

Boyish good looks and serious acting chops only took you so far in the entertainment industry, however. What really set Dolian Crawford apart was the veil of mystery in which he remained cloaked. No one knew anything about his personal life. He rarely gave interviews, always attended events alone, and had never once been photographed with another person. While his co-stars always spoke highly and reverently of his talent and professionalism, it was like Dolian Crawford ceased to exist the moment he stepped off camera.

It all only heightened his sex appeal to Imogen, not that she would ever admit that out loud. More than one person had referred to it as an obsession. Her mother even went so far as to accuse Imogen of stalking.

Was it "stalking" if she kept a binder under her bed of every news article his name had ever been in? Perhaps.

Was it "obsession" that she looked up all of the property deeds in the Los Angeles area under the name of his agent, assistant, and publicist so that she had a rough estimate of where he lived? Probably.

Was it "fanaticism" that she frequently chose to work in overpriced cafes and bistros in that area to see if she *accidentally* encountered him and proved her hunch correct? More than likely.

But Imogen had so few joys in life at the moment that she allowed herself a harmless little crush. She wasn't like one of those crazy, obsessive fans people read about on the internet. She was different. Innocent. Nothing worth fretting over.

As the lights grew brighter and the hum of activity grew louder, Imogen emerged in the press pen. Journalists stayed in a separate area from fans along the entrance to the red carpet so that they could have a quick word with the actors on their way in. Only fifty or so members of the press had been invited to the premiere, and Imogen thanked Lady Fortune again for winning the press badge through an internet contest. An anonymous email sent it to her inbox, which seemed suspicious up until she won. Now, she was over the moon with excitement and adrenaline.

Paparazzi and photographers had a separate station where a backdrop with the film's title was present. Signs were posted in the area discouraging photographs, but there was only one security guard stationed in the opposite corner. One little selfie couldn't possibly matter.

However, as Imogen held up her cell to capture the screaming fans in the shot behind her, security materialized out of nowhere, knocking the phone right out of her hand. The screen shattered as it hit the concrete...an accident Imogen could *not* afford.

"Oh no!" she cried. "What have you done?!" Bending down, she scooped up the remnants of her phone, a six year old iPhone that a neighbor jailbroke for her, as tears sprang to her eyes. It was a total loss; none of the screen was visible now. Why oh why did she let Austin take her phone case?!

"You WILL pay to replace that," a gravelly voice stated at Imogen's back. "And your services will no longer be required here."

Slowly, she rose to an upright position and turned to thank her savior...only to find none other than Dolian Crawford himself appraising her. His eyes were so blue they were nearly gray, and they held an intensity that sent a small sliver of fear trailing down her spine. She didn't know what to make of it.

Words failed her—having the object of your schoolgirl crush in front of you will do that—and it took several seconds for Imogen to remember to clamp her mouth shut. Heat flooded her cheeks, the space suddenly agonizingly hot, and she wiped one sweaty palm as innocuously as possible on the hem of her dress.

Dolian, however, smiled at her. "Are you alright?"

She nodded mutely, her eyes darting back to her shoes as she battled her internal panic.

He turned back to the security guard, his gravelly voice suddenly harsh and cold. "You will provide Ms. Reilly with a brand new iPhone, complete with a protective case, before the night is through, and then you will return to the security station. Watching computer monitors is clearly all you are fit for."

Imogen glanced up and noted the guard was trembling. "Yes, Mr. Crawford. Right away, Mr. Crawford. I'm so sorry, ma'am!" He scampered away like a child fleeing the boogeyman. If Imogen didn't know any better, she would almost say he was terrified. But who could be terrified of Dolian Crawford?

In a daze, she turned back to him, eyes wide and uncertain. While it ruined her night to have her phone destroyed, this was singlehandedly the most exhilarating thing to ever happen to her. *The* Dolian Crawford stood up for her like a gallant knight defending her honor. No one had ever done something like that for Imogen before.

He seemed to sense she was more than a little awestruck,

asking her again like he might have asked a child, "Are you sure you're okay?" Dolian's strong hand gripped her elbow. The touch was the only thing keeping Imogen grounded.

"My name?" she whispered. "How did you know my name?"

Dolian's smile dropped for barely a moment before he explained, "It's on your press badge, of course."

By that time, several other journalists hovered around them, watching their exchange with keen interest. Imogen blinked several times to gather her wits about her. She gently tugged her elbow from his hold. Perhaps it was her overactive imagination that the action made him frown. It was there and gone in a flash.

Evette Coleman, the lead anchor on *Movie News Now*, an entertainment-focused evening news show, sidled over. Her long blonde hair dangled in perfect beachy-waves and her sparkly hi-lo dress fit her like a glove, the rich purple color illuminating her bronzed skin. On any other day, being that close to an entertainment journalist as famous as Evette Coleman would have sent Imogen in a tailspin. But standing next to Dolian Crawford dazzled her far too much to care.

"Well, that was a close call, huh?!" Evette's gaze ping-ponged between the two of them, assessing their interaction like a hawk aiming to dive. "Thank God you were here to save the day, Dolian!" Long, blood red nails in the perfect acrylic manicure ever so slightly stroked his arm as she batted her thick eyelashes at him.

Dolian, however, did not take his eyes off Imogen. "I must insist that you stay close to me inside the theater," he said. "I have to make sure he honors his agreement to replace your phone."

Imogen swallowed thickly and tried to get a handle on her rapidly beating heart. "I—I'll be fine," she replied. "Thank you for helping me, Mr. Crawford."

He smiled again, showcasing gleaming white teeth that were straight, even, and symmetrical. Truly, it was a smile almost too perfect to be real. "Please, call me Dolian. Enjoy the film."

As he sauntered away towards the waiting crowd of fans along the red carpet and the line of paparazzi eager to take a shot from his best angle, the actor was as poised and captivating as always. Yet Imogen regarded him with new eyes. The spot on her elbow where he touched her still tingled as though her very skin buzzed with the memory of his skin on hers.

"So where are you from?" Evette asked, her voice no longer dripping with honey, but with a heavy Boston accent.

Imogen kept her eyes on Dolian's retreating form. "Compton," she answered.

Evette snorted. "No, like what news outlet." Her disdain was apparent.

"Oh, yeah, sorry. I run a celebrity gossip blog called *Hollywood Unmasked*." Imogen held out a hand to introduce herself. "Hi, I'm Imogen Reilly."

Her companion merely glanced at her proffered hand before snorting again. "Wow, they'll just let anyone into these things now," commented Evette. Several other people nearby snickered. "Go home, Compton Barbie."

She spun on her heel, not even teetering in her sky high stilettos. Imogen would fall and break an ankle if she tried to walk in shoes like that. Life simply wasn't fair sometimes.

Bullies were nothing new for her, having grown up her

entire life being smaller than most of her classmates. There was nothing imposing about Imogen, nothing that made anyone consider her much of a rival, let alone a threat. Poverty always kept her thin while genetics kept her short.

Yet to hear someone in the industry, whom she had always looked up to, make her feel so inferior struck a nerve. She wanted nothing more than to wilt into the shadows. Awareness of how much her vintage dress and scuffed platform shoes stood out dyed her cheeks a vibrant scarlet. While Evette Coleman's makeup was flawlessly applied by a professional, Imogen swiped dollar store mascara on and called it a day. She had no business trying to break into the industry by attending the summer's blockbuster movie premiere.

Shame set her cheeks aflame again, and she turned forlornly towards the exit. Imogen hadn't even hit the hallway before a large man in a black suit stepped in front of her path. His face was heavily scarred...and scowling at her.

"This way," he ordered, gesturing in the opposite direction.

"Excuse me?" Imogen asked. "Who are you?"

"Mr. Crawford wants you to join him in the theater," the man answered. Imogen had to crane her neck back to take him all in. He had to have been a boxer in another life, although the marks on his face suggested he lost a fight a time or two.

"Do you work for Dolian Crawford?" Imogen asked. She knew his agent was an older woman named Maude Clemmings, an old Hollywood darling whose last successful client fell out of favor in the '80s. His assistant and his publicist were also identified as women, according to his website.

The man didn't respond, merely gestured again in the opposite direction.

Imogen was too intrigued to argue. The allure of learning something new about the movie star was too great to ignore. He fell into step beside her, placing a heavy hand in the middle of her back to steer her towards their destination…or to prevent Imogen from leaving. She wasn't entirely sure which.

The fans along the red carpet were shrieking at higher decibels than Imogen would have thought possible. None of the actors posing for the photographers or signing autographs seemed phased. Dolian smiled politely and waved to the young girls behind the gate screaming his name, but Imogen noted wryly that it was a thin, tight smile rather than the dazzling one he gave her. Nobody noticed as the man in black wove them through the crowd of the press box, behind the giant movie posters, and into the lobby of the Westwood theater.

As the man headed towards the emergency door at the back of the lobby, however, Imogen started digging in her heels. "Wait a minute!" she exclaimed. "Where are you taking me?! Who are you?!"

Imogen frantically spun and prepared to bolt, only to run into a hard chest. Firm hands circled around her biceps to lock her in place.

"There you are, Ms. Reilly," Dolian Crawford said, peering down at her with a grin. "Let's find our seats. Thank you, Huxley." He nodded over her shoulder at the man in black before circling an arm around her waist to pull her tight against his hip.

The other people in the lobby outright gawked. More than

one person had their mouths hanging open in shock. Dolian had *never* been seen with a woman, yet clearly had his arm around her. Imogen sent a silent prayer of thanks that photographers weren't allowed inside because while she wanted to report on the entertainment industry, she had no desire to have her face splashed across the tabloids.

If Dolian noticed the attention, he did not seem to show it. Instead, he held open the door to the theater for her, waving her through like a dandy, and chuckled at the flush that crept across her cheeks. Imogen idly wondered if it was possible to permanently turn red from embarrassment.

"So, Ms. Reilly," he said as they made their way to seats in the front row, "are you looking forward to the film?"

"Oh—um. Yes?" Imogen had always fantasized about meeting Dolian and sweeping him off his feet with how cool and unimpressed she was by his stardom, appearing in her dreams as a much more sophisticated version of herself. It was all entirely untrue in the moment; Imogen couldn't remember how to make her mouth function other than monosyllables.

Dolian smiled easily at her, as though he found her flustered state charming. "I have to be honest with you." He leaned in conspiratorially to whisper in her ear. "We filmed it so long ago that I can barely remember the plot! Or maybe it's just your perfume." The edge of his nose danced against the spot where her jaw met her earlobe. "You smell divine."

Right now, it's about ninety percent sweat, thought Imogen.

"Thank you," she murmured instead. It all felt too surreal to be true, and she fought the urge to fidget with her hands. Demurely, glancing up at him through her eyelashes, Imogen noted the way his breath caught and his eyes darkened as he looked at her.

"Do you really want to see the movie? Maybe we could go talk somewhere more private?" Even Dolian's hopeful whisper made her stomach erupt with butterflies.

Imogen didn't trust herself to speak. Hell, she could barely manage to breathe, given the circumstances. She nodded, then tried not to swoon when Dolian's hand laced through hers.

Back in the lobby, Imogen dropped his hand like it burned her as soon as Evette Coleman's eyes landed on them. One delicately manicured eyebrow rose in challenge as she sauntered over.

"My, you two certainly have a way of finding one another," Evette quipped. It was meant to be playful, but only sounded bitter to Imogen's ears. "Do you know each other?"

"I was actually about to give Ms. Reilly an exclusive interview," Dolian replied smoothly. It was a natural movement, one that would not have garnered attention to anyone else, but he subtly adjusted the weight on his feet so that his body shifted away from Evette and closer to Imogen. He then wrapped an arm around her waist again.

Evette zeroed in on the arm before letting out a fake laugh. "But Dolian, you never give interviews! Everybody knows that!" She swatted his arm playfully as if they were in on a joke together.

He shrugged. "I give interviews to the right people."

It was a respectful insult, and judging by the way Evette's smile dropped, she knew it. "Perhaps you should refine your taste," Evette suggested, eyeing Imogen up and down again in a way that had all her insecurities roaring in the back of her mind.

Imogen pulled herself from Dolian's embrace, scared of the repercussions if either of them noticed the tears forming in her eyes. "I have to go," she excused herself quickly.

Her feet had wings as she powerwalked through the throng of people congregating in the lobby, no longer caring about the impression she gave as she pushed them out of the way. Her tears were about to fall any second and she didn't want to give Evette Coleman the satisfaction of seeing her victory.

The man in black from earlier tried to intercede, but she managed to dodge him in her haste to get outside. She could hear Dolian Crawford calling for her at her back.

Imogen didn't stop until she reached her bus stop five blocks away. It would take her more than two hours to get home, including changing over to a new bus that would take her all the way out to Compton. It wasn't until she took her seat on the bus, in the very last row by the window, sinking down as far as the sturdy plastic chair allowed, that she finally let the tears fall.

Humiliating. That's what the night turned into, at the drop of a hat. She had no business trying to break into the entertainment business, even if it was as a low level blogger. Most people starting out in Los Angeles had some sort of connection, an inside track from a friend's uncle or their hairdresser's cousin, but she had no one. Her mom worked three jobs just to pay their rent, leaving Imogen at home to care for Austin. It was really her love for Dolian Crawford that spurred her towards a celebrity gossip blog. Doing something from home that could earn money and had the potential to get her closer to her idol seemed like a no brainer—and now Imogen couldn't remember a single reason why.

But the way he *looked* at her! Smiling in such a way that Imogen knew it to be genuine, touching her arm, leaning into her ear to whisper…those hadn't been figments of her imagination. It made Imogen's heart race and her stomach quicken. Even if Evette Coleman's insults were accurate—maybe she really didn't belong in Hollywood—nothing could take the feel of Dolian's breath on her neck in that theater, however brief.

While the memory of the night might make her shudder with embarrassment, Imogen never wanted to forget that for a split second, Dolian Crawford, A-list international movie star, wanted to speak to her *privately*. It was almost too fantastical to believe.

THREE

"I mean, what's he hiding anyway? Does Dolian Crawford really need to be such a hermit?"
-Howard Stern radio

"Welcome home," her mom said as Imogen slipped through the front door. She set the deadbolt locks and chain locks, not that they had anything of value to steal in their tiny apartment.

"Thanks, Mom. How was Austin?" she asked.

Her mother, Sylvia Reilly, was already in faded scrubs for her night job as a caregiver at the nursing home in Long Beach. It had been a huge request to have her mom take an evening off from her afternoon job at the convenience store below their apartment. Working there gave the family a discount on their rent. Their landlord owned the store, too.

"He's in his room." Sylvia waved a hand dismissively. "I couldn't stand the banging."

Imogen dug her fingernails into her palms to prevent the scathing retort from leaving her mouth. Her mom's continual disdain for her younger brother's condition drove her mad. Down Syndrome wasn't something to brush off, nor was it a lifestyle choice, as her mother often acted. Like Austin actively sat and considered whether his quirks were annoying just to piss her off.

Austin had always been Imogen's biggest motivator since the day he was born. At only four, Imogen still remembered looking at the tiny bundle in wonder and awe, determined to protect him. She was already acutely aware of how the world would turn against him for being different. Unfortunately, more often than not, that meant protecting Austin from their mother, whose patience and compassion seemed to be reserved for her patients at the nursing home more than her own son.

Some people with Down Syndrome never fully learn to speak, which happened to be the case for Austin. He relied heavily on pictures to communicate as he could identify his needs better by pointing to things like a bathroom rather than saying he needed to use it. Imogen spent so much time with him now that she could almost interpret the meaning behind some of his grunts or monosyllabic responses, a talent their mother never bothered to master. Therefore, whenever Imogen had to leave for extended periods where Austin couldn't go to the day center for adults with disabilities, he tended to grow frustrated with their mom's lack of understanding and resorted to repetitive behaviors like banging on walls or stomping his feet, called stimming. It always pissed Sylvia off, and no matter how many times

Imogen tried to explain what she could do differently, she never tried.

"I'll go take care of him," she said now. "Have a good night at work."

Sylvia nodded her thanks. "There's some pizza left in the fridge if you want to eat anything. Lock up behind me!"

Imogen sighed. The pizza was likely the culprit of Austin's banging as he liked eating the cheese separately. Imogen knew that and peeled it off to put on an extra plate whereas their mom refused, saying it dirtied too many dishes. It was always laughable to Imogen because she was the one who had to wash all the dishes anyway. Why should Sylvia care if there was one more?

She found her brother in his bedroom, sitting on the floor in front of the television and rocking so that his head hit the mattress of the bed behind him. It was a tiny room, with just enough space for a twin bed, a plastic chest of drawers with a tv precariously perched on top, and a bookcase with two shelves. Austin liked snow globes, so Imogen filled the bookcase with as many as she could find when she scoured garage sales and flea markets.

He jumped up now and clapped, a bright smile illuminating his face at the sight of her. Imogen grinned and Austin swallowed her in a hug.

"I know, I missed you, too, buddy," she said. His banging now moved to her back, quick thumps with the palm of his hand that signified his excitement but also his anxiety at her having left. "Yeah, I'm sorry about the pizza. Can I take the cheese off for you?"

Austin nodded and gave her a toothy smile. It warmed her heart to see.

Imogen had only just gotten Austin settled in the living room with pizza and a superhero movie when a knock pounded on the door. It was late and they didn't have any friends who would stop by. Nobody wanted to hurt themselves on the five floor walkup. It was also a good prevention from the meth addicts that tended to roam the area.

Her heart began to race when the knock came again. Even Austin sat up straighter, turning towards the door and pointing frantically. With his show as loud as it was and the light shining underneath the door, Imogen couldn't exactly play it off as no one was home. She slowly edged towards the door, trying to angle her body so that there weren't any shadows to prove she was checking through the peep hole.

Because their landlord was such a cheapskate, however, the lightbulbs in the hallway had never been replaced. The person on the other side of the door wore a dark hat that obscured his face and what looked like a hoodie with the hood pulled up over the hat. He held a small box in his hand.

Imogen jumped when he pounded on the door a third time with far more aggression. "Who's there?" she called out in a shaky voice.

"I've got a package to deliver!" His voice was a deep baritone, one she didn't recognize.

"We aren't expecting any packages!" shouted Imogen. Her heart now beat in her throat, and she pushed both hands against the door as though preparing for the man to barge in as she continued to watch him through the peep hole.

He threw up his hands. "Look, lady, this guy at the theater paid me a shitload of money to deliver this phone to Imogen Reilly! I'm not missing out on that cash, so you better take it!"

The guy at the theater? Surely Dolian didn't still care about her phone!

Hesitantly, Imogen unlocked the two deadbolts, but left the chain locks on so she could only open the door an inch, at most. A young Latino male stood outside with a look of impatience. From the tiny shaft of light casting over her shoulder, Imogen realized that his pants and shoes matched those of the valet at the movie premiere.

"Are you Imogen Reilly?" the man asked her pointedly.

She nodded.

"Then here!" He angrily shoved the box through the gap in the door and spun on his heel to go down the stairs.

Imogen took the box over to the rickety kitchen table and used a knife to slice open the packaging. Inside was a brand new iPhone in a sparkly green Otterbox case, complete with matching popsocket, charging cord, and a camera attachment.

Austin came over and started clapping at the sight of the phone. He pointed animatedly, saying, "Call! Call!"

She smiled at him. "Yeah, bud, I can call again." But in the pit of her stomach, dread seeped in. *How did Dolian Crawford get her address?*

As if on cue, a text came through the phone, illuminating the screen and vibrating in her hand. Shocked, Imogen jumped and dropped the phone on the ground.

"Thank god for the case, huh?" she asked Austin with a breathy laugh.

Austin smiled before returning to the living room.

The text was from a number she didn't recognize. It read,

> Mr. Crawford will meet with you at 10
> tomorrow morning at the following address:

When Imogen pulled up the location on Google maps, it looked to be deep in the Topatopa Mountains well outside of the L.A. County jurisdiction. There wouldn't be a bus line that could take her that far.

Again, it was like her thoughts summoned the next text that came through.

> A car will be waiting for you downstairs.

She didn't know whether to laugh or cry. An exclusive with the most notoriously private movie star in the world would *definitely* put her on everybody's radar. It would create a media storm like no other, and Imogen would no doubt feel the financial ramifications for a lifetime.

Yet, something about the entire situation terrified her. How did he manage to find her home address? That wasn't something a security officer could have pulled up along with her press badge. And everything was under her mom's name anyway, which Dolian Crawford couldn't have known. Something about his insistence needled her. It should have been an alarm.

But as Imogen glanced over at Austin, who sat on the sagging sofa watching one of the handful of DVD's she bought him at garage sales as a means of entertainment, she realized there was really no choice. Money like that would be a game changer for Austin, and Imogen wanted nothing more than to take him out of their mother's minuscule apartment and into a better part of the Valley. Somewhere that he could be safe and have all of his needs met.

So she ignored all the warning sirens in her head as she typed out,

Okay.

FOUR

"Dolian Crawford, renown for being extremely private about his personal life, declined to comment at this time."
-Josie Whitaker, Good Day USA anchor

The next morning started off on the wrong foot from the moment Imogen opened her eyes. Austin hadn't slept well, needing a breathing treatment for the mucus buildup in his lungs. Normally he had a dehumidifier in his room, but it broke the week prior and despite their mom's reassurance that she could bring an old one from the nursing home, Imogen's reminders to do so had been ignored. It made Austin crabbier than usual and he started banging loudly on the walls when Imogen explained that he had to go to the day center because she had an appointment.

Ever since Austin graduated high school last year, Imogen enrolled him in a day program for people with disabilities. Her hope was that he could learn enough of a skill that he could work part time and find a sense of fulfillment outside of their apartment. It was also important that he made friends who looked and acted like him so that he didn't feel isolated as adults with Down Syndrome often did. Most days, he loved it and Imogen felt relieved to find a place where Austin was so openly accepted and well-treated.

But when he was in a bad mood from lack of sleep, no one except Imogen could soothe him. He was crabby the entire way to the day center and refused to go inside. She had to coax him with a candy bar, a treat that he was normally forbidden from eating because he made such a mess with the chocolate. Austin preferred letting it melt in his hands and then using the chocolate to finger paint on whatever surface was closest at the time. Thankfully one of the staff members at the center sensed her frustrations and distracted Austin enough that she could slip out the front door. She barely made it in time for the bus back to her house, but then her real worries began.

Her mom dozed on the couch, which also served as her bed since she was so rarely home. Imogen tried to move silently through the apartment to take a shower and get ready, but as soon as she stepped behind the shower curtain, she heard Sylvia from the doorway.

"Where is Austin?" her mom asked.

"I had to take him to the day center," Imogen called out over the heavy shower stream. "I have an interview for the blog."

"Imogen, it's time you grow up!" Sylvia snapped angrily. "You need a real job so you can pay bills! I shouldn't be the one providing for you anymore!"

It was the same fight they always had. And yet, Sylvia never acknowledged the elephant in the room, that somebody had to stay home with Austin and insurance paid for Imogen to do so. Not that Imogen ever saw a dime of that money. Everything was deposited into Sylvia's bank account. She would begrudgingly give Imogen some of her cash tips after working her shifts at the diner so that Imogen wasn't destitute.

"And what about Austin?" Imogen turned off the water in an angry huff, snatching the towel off the hook on the wall and wrapping it around herself to face her mother head on. "He can't be here by himself, Mom, you know that!"

Sylvia rolled her eyes. "We can't take care of him, Imogen! I told you, he needs to go to a home!"

Imogen shoved past her, too livid to speak. She hated it when her mother brought this up. A friend of Sylvia's found a group home near Glendale that took in adults with Down Syndrome and Sylvia wouldn't shut up about it. She thought it was the perfect solution because it meant Austin was no longer their burden to carry and would require somebody else to maintain his daily needs. Not that Sylvia ever took care of those anyway.

Her mother only followed her across the hall.

"It's time that you grow up, little girl!" Sylvia continued. "You can't keep chasing after movie stars like Dolian Crawford and ignoring your responsibilities! You need to get out of my house and start providing for yourself!"

Imogen flushed as she rounded on her. "That's what I'm trying to do, Mom! Take care of myself AND take care of Austin! How can you even think about sending him to live with strangers?!"

She moved around the room, the larger of the two bedrooms in the apartment, with a closet and chest of drawers for clothes that Imogen had to share with Sylvia. Any other time, Imogen would analyze her outfit, desperate to make a better impression on Dolian than she managed yesterday. Today she only focused on grabbing whatever was clean and fit right.

"Don't you need to be at work?" Imogen finally asked. They would only fight in circles until one of them had to leave.

Sylvia scowled at her. "Of course I do! I work myself to the bone—unlike you!" And with that, she stomped through the apartment, slamming the front door on her way out.

Wearily, Imogen sank onto the misshapen mattress with a heavy sigh. Writing about Hollywood was the only thing she could think of to be *in* Hollywood and keep herself available to care for Austin. As long as she continued to utilize the day center to keep him busy and active during business hours, it shouldn't matter that she allowed herself the freedom to pursue her gossip blog. Influencers could make serious money nowadays, so why couldn't Imogen have a slice of that pie?

A text on her phone beeped to let her know that the car was waiting downstairs. She hastily braided her pale brown hair into a thin plait over her shoulder and took one last look in the full length mirror hanging over the back of the door. While her face was clammy from anger, Imogen thought her outfit was otherwise acceptable. A simple V-neck, gray shirt paired with a thick black belt and a white jean mini skirt. Dolian always favored gray suits. She would match his style.

Imogen slipped on a pair of black wedge sandals and pushed her cat-eye sunglasses onto her face. It would be well over an hour drive, so she would have plenty of time to put on makeup in the car. Whether she liked it or not, the look would have to do. She was already running late.

A slender Asian man stood at the back passenger door of a sleek BMW sedan. He even sported a little black cap like chauffeurs from another century. Despite Imogen's greeting, the man remained silent as he waved her inside the vehicle and closed the door with a snap behind her.

To her surprise, there was a solid black partition between the front and back seats. She heard the driver door open and close, and then they were off.

It suddenly dawned on her that this could be a bad idea. Nobody knew where she was headed, although she doubted Sylvia would have believed her if she told her. Imogen rarely kept in touch with any of her old friends since most of them had gone on to work full time or had babies of their own.

Use this time productively! the voice in her head ordered.

Imogen decided to write down some questions for Dolian, ranging from lighthearted to intimately comprehensive. If she was going to write the first ever exclusive interview on the world's biggest celebrity, she wanted to get all the gory details out in the open.

After compiling a list of questions on Dolian's personal life and some generic questions about the movie (since she never got to see it last night), Imogen started aimlessly looking through the apps already installed on her phone. This version of an iPhone had way more bells and whistles than her previous phone. Somehow, she landed on a news app where several major headlines caught her attention.

"ENTERTAINMENT NEWS ANCHOR SLAIN"
"THE WORLD REELS FROM HOLLYWOOD MURDER"

"EVETTE COLEMAN: KILLED IN COLD BLOOD"

Imogen's eyes nearly blurred from how quickly she began reading. Evette Coleman, the scathingly critical reporter from the premiere, had been found dead in her Brentwood home when her Pilates instructor arrived that morning for their usual training session. Officials ruled her death a homicide and were actively investigating, though the autopsy report could take up to sixteen weeks.

"Oh my god!" She couldn't remember how to breathe. The whole thing was just too unsettling, given their unpleasant exchange at the theater last night. Imogen had known death from a young age; their neighborhood in Compton had its fair share of drive by's, gang fights, and drug addicts. Checking the obituaries was as routine as brushing her teeth.

So why did Evette's feel so...personal? Imogen couldn't stop picturing Evette's ugly sneer, the way that her hand possessively touched Dolian's arm, or the way everyone in the lobby stared at her like a freak circus sideshow when Evette pointed out how much Imogen didn't fit in. Last night had been a disaster, at best, but Imogen never wanted her *dead*.

Sources in all the articles claimed that Evette hadn't been seen since the *Agent Reckless* movie premiere. Somewhere in the time between the premiere and her six a.m. workout session, she had been murdered.

Imogen forgot all about her makeup as she spent the rest of the drive combing through articles, video footage, and her favorite gossip influencers discussing Evette's death. Conspiracy theories were rampant as the journalist had a habit of grilling Hollywood starlets to the point that she made enemies. Imogen read through dozens upon dozens of articles before any of them made mention of her encounter with Evette at the premiere last night, and even then it only identified her as an "unknown blogger seen with Dolian Crawford."

Whew! That was a relief! Imogen wanted to report *on* the entertainment news, not *be* the entertainment news. And as much as she wanted her blog to take off, Imogen always imagined it as a gradually steady influx of subscribers. Becoming an overnight sensation could prove to be overwhelming. Especially to Austin. She shuddered to think of how he would react to the drastic changes that would come their way if that happened.

Before long, the cell service began to grow spotty, so the last thing Imogen read was another much smaller article about another man found murdered in an alleyway in West Hollywood, near the theater that held the *Agent Reckless* premiere. Service faded away entirely just as Imogen read that the man worked for the security company in charge of the premiere and had been identified as Jesse Ramirez. She couldn't scroll any further to read more after that.

This news rattled her just as much as headlines over Evette Coleman. What were the odds that two different people were killed after attending the same event? The itch to see a photograph of the guard was enough to make her palms sweaty. If it was the same man who bumped into her and destroyed her cell phone, Dolian could be implicated as he had been seen with both victims in their final hours. Imogen needed to warn him!

She stressed over it for the remainder of the drive. Even

the scenic forest they drove through did nothing to distract her. It could very well be a false alarm, but when it came to Dolian Crawford, she would take nothing to chance. There had never been a scandal attached to his name and Imogen didn't want one to start now.

By the time the BMW pulled up to a tall, black gate, Imogen's anxiety had created a veritable shit storm in her mind. She pictured all the media outlets labeling Dolian as a person of interest, suggesting his private nature might actually hide something far more sinister. As much as the press loved him now, it could all change in the blink of an eye. They were fickle that way.

Imogen was so lost in her imaginings that she didn't notice that the driver needed to type in a numeric passcode and submit to a retinal scan to open the gate. Nor did she catch the thickness of the gate itself, black metal heavy enough to withstand a battering ram. The gate and the surrounding metal fence were over ten feet high.

The car followed a winding driveway further up the mountain where the trees grew thicker. Several large ravens cawed coyly from the trees, finally earning Imogen's attention. Just when she was about to knock on the partition to ask the driver how much higher the car could climb, a gargantuan stone mansion emerged through the trees. It looked as though the very mountain craigs had been carved into a Gothic structure fit for Bram Stoker himself. Although the sun peered brightly overhead, something made her pause before stepping out of the car as it drew to a stop in the circular drive. The air was thinner at this altitude, colder, and she had the irrational sense that something sinister lurked about. Imogen repressed a shiver as she accepted the chauffeur's proffered hand.

Nobody was visible in any of the windows, yet she had the uncanny feeling that she was being watched. The chauffeur still remained silent. He only gestured with his arm towards the front door before returning to his vehicle, which then drove back down the drive and turned off onto a secondary drive that curved around the side of the mountain, and therefore the house.

Imogen gulped before approaching the door. Right as she raised her hand to knock, the ornate wood door opened. The same man in the same black suit as the movie premiere stood before her. "Huxley" if she recalled his name correctly.

"Hi," she offered with a small wave. "I am here to see Dolian Crawford."

He nodded and opened the door even wider. She found herself in a circular, three story foyer, complete with a multi-tiered crystal chandelier. The floors were made of a rich mahogany, but the walls maintained the same stony façade as the exterior of the home. A marble table stood directly under the chandelier and sported a China vase with the biggest roses Imogen had ever seen. Despite the size of the home, the foyer felt small in comparison, with several closed doors on the wall. Once Huxley closed the front door it was impossible to tell which was which. She wouldn't know how to find her way out. It made the hairs on the back of her neck stand up.

"Ms. Reilly!" Dolian himself entered through a door to her left, wearing a smile wide enough to showcase his dimples. He had on a snowy white henley shirt that fit him like a second skin and a pair of navy slacks. Imogen momentarily lost her breath as she took in his wide, muscular shoulders and lean waist. Dolian aged like a fine wine; she was still as attracted to him now as she had been as a young teenager.

"H-hello, Mr. C-crawford!" she stuttered back.

He stopped before her, his smile now towering over her in a dazzling array of perfect teeth. "Do we really need to be so formal with each other? How about I call you 'Imogen' and you call me 'Dolian.' Like friends!" he added while looping her arm around his. "You *are* the first person to ever grace the halls of my little villa!"

As he led them down a long stone corridor, complete with flickering wall sconces, Imogen had to fight back a snort. "Little villa" indeed!

The pair emerged in an enormous two story room that looked half atrium, half cave. Two of the walls appeared to be carved right into the mountain side, the gray rock weathered and warped. The other two walls were made entirely out of glass. It provided a panoramic view of a garden maze winding down the mountainside. Plush roses, a rich scarlet, bloomed on all of the bushes that melted into the tree line on both sides.

Yet the most impressive feature of all was the in ground infinity pool that began halfway into the room, then extended under the glass and for several feet outside before dropping abruptly off the edge. Imogen wondered if it created a waterfall outside.

Closer to the cave wall, a seating area of brown leather couches and oversized chairs centered around a glass coffee table piled high with scripts and books. An open galley kitchen ran along the glass wall opposite them. Olive green cabinets and rustic wooden beams holding cookware somehow blended into the feel of the place. At the end of the kitchen, a wrought iron staircase led up to a balcony of sorts that jutted out above the couches. It led to four wooden doors that matched the ones found in the foyer, carved into the rock. All were shut.

As discreetly as possible, Imogen reached down to pinch her thigh. There was no way she could have dreamed up something this spectacular, but yet it seemed too grand to be real.

"Welcome to my home, Imogen," Dolian said, sweeping his arm around as if presenting it to her. "I hope you'll be very happy here."

She gulped. That was an odd thing to say. "It's a great place to conduct an interview."

Was it her imagination or did Dolian frown at her response? All too quickly, his smile returned, though it didn't quite reach his eyes. "Yes. An interview. Would you like something to drink? I'll make us brunch as soon as the gardeners bring in what they've gathered."

Imogen gasped. "You grow your own food?"

Dolian shrugged. "It's easier than grocery shopping."

"And *you* are going to cook it? For *me*?"

The movie star smiled wider. "It's my pleasure to do this for you. I know how exhausting that drive can be. I'm grateful you were willing to come all the way out here."

He moved into the kitchen and withdrew a tall bottle of sparkling water from the refrigerator before grabbing two glasses off a hanging shelf over the island countertop. Pouring the water into both glasses, he pushed one towards Imogen and drank deeply from his own. "Let's go out onto the terrace," Dolian suggested.

Imogen followed him around the edge of the pool and carefully inched closer to the wall so that her hand could trace the metal joint of the window. Dolian glanced back over his shoulder at her, then paused.

"Is everything okay?" he asked.

Her cheeks burned. It had to be a record for how often she managed to embarrass herself in the presence of her celebrity crush. "I can't swim. After a bad accident in my childhood where I learned how quickly someone could drown, I don't like going near any kind of water."

Like a switch flipped, Imogen's thoughts drifted back to that day.

It was a particularly hot day in late July, and Imogen and Austin were at their babysitter's apartment. She felt old enough to conquer the world at only eight, while Austin still seemed like such a baby to her at four. Their sitter that summer was the mother of a friend of a friend of Sylvia's, and whenever she wanted to watch a movie or show she deemed inappropriate for the two of them, she sent them outside to play in the apartment complex's courtyard.

On that particular day, Imogen watched as one of the neighbor kids, probably a few years older than her, walked around to a gate at the back of the apartment where there was an in ground pool. The kid lifted a latch on the other side of the gate to push it open, then ran inside to cannon ball into the bright blue water. There were already other kids swimming, though only one or two adults were visible in chaise lounges, tanning.

Even though they didn't have swimsuits, Imogen thought sticking their feet in the water might still help them cool off. She grabbed Austin's sticky hand and all but dragged him over to the gate. Austin struggled with mobility and walking was difficult for him. By four, he still hadn't managed to run properly. But Imogen's impatience wasn't going to be held up by a toddler.

Once inside the gate, nobody gave them a second glance. Imogen eagerly ran to the shallow end, where they could sit on the edge and let their feet rest on the steps. She flung off her sandals before peeling Austin's off, too, shoving his bottom down so that he could sit.

The water wasn't nearly as cold as she expected it to be. Why did it look like such an icy shade of blue if it was going to feel more like bathwater? *she wondered. Maybe she just wasn't in far enough.*

Since they were on the steps and her shorts were high enough that she could submerge more of her leg, Imogen stood up and descended onto the next stair. If she hiked up her shorts a little more, she could almost make it to the third step. No matter how high she tugged, however, it wasn't enough for her to feel any cold water. She didn't feel an ounce of relief from the heat.

A loud splash came from behind, and Imogen turned to find Austin tried to follow her. Only he was too small and wasn't used to walking at all, let alone walking with the waves of a swimming pool. He tumbled into the water, hands and legs failing.

"AUSTIN!" Imogen screamed. No matter how hard she tugged at his arms, Austin couldn't right himself. She didn't have the upper body strength to lift him.

One of the adults from the chaise lounge ran over and plucked a squalling Austin from the water.

"What are you trying to pull, kid?!" the man screamed at her. He pounded on her brother's back, holding him with his head down to force the water to come out. Poor Austin sputtered and screamed as water poured from his mouth, coughing harshly.

Imogen's tears were so heavy, they blurred her vision. Once the man set Austin down on his feet, she crushed her brother to her chest, sobbing hysterically to everyone in the vicinity about how sorry she was.

Sylvia was livid when the sitter called to tell her they were all at the hospital after Austin had an accident. Imogen had to relive the terror over and over again as she explained what happened to multiple doctors, nurses, the sitter, and then their mother. In the end, Austin was okay, but they never went back to that sitter again.

And Imogen stopped entering any kind of water beyond that of a shower.

Thankfully, Dolian didn't press her to share details on where her brain wandered. He merely came around to stand between her and the pool, like a human shield, and guided her through the glass door to a stone terrace that jutted around the edge of the mansion. There was no door handle that Imogen could see. Somehow Dolian just knew where to push and the panel opened into a door.

Judging by the sound of the water falling from the pool, it created a waterfall of sorts, but Imogen didn't have a chance to look over. Dolian guided her over to a glass table underneath a large hunter green umbrella. The air smelled fragrant, the balcony walls adorned with boxes of jasmine and brightly colored poppies. It was a paradise to someone like Imogen, who never had an outdoor space to utilize.

"Did you hear about Evette Coleman?" Imogen asked.

Dolian paused as he sat down across from her, glancing out to the garden before looking back at her. "I haven't," he replied. "What about Evette Coleman?"

"She was murdered! Sometime after attending the *Agent Reckless* premiere!" Imogen waited with bated breath for his response.

"How unfortunate." Yet there wasn't a trace of remorse in his statement.

Dolian nodded to someone over her shoulder, and Imogen turned to see Huxley holding a tray with another bottle of sparkling water and their glasses. He brought them to the table, serving them both, before leaving the bottle in a small cooler of ice just behind Dolian's elbow. Huxley gave his employer a subtle bow before returning inside.

"Who is that?" Imogen had to know. There was something about Huxley that made her break out in goosebumps.

"Huxley?" Dolian asked as though genuinely confused by her question. "He's my right hand man, so to speak. A jack of all trades, really. Everyone and everything goes through him; I wouldn't be here today without him."

And yet his very existence was news to Imogen, who had been following Dolian's career as closely as possible for nearly a decade. No one had ever breathed a word of an assistant who served as a gatekeeper to all things Dolian Crawford.

Imogen frowned at this new piece of information. "Is that why you've never done an interview?"

The movie star's eyes darkened. "We're conducting an interview now, are we not?"

"Oh, I didn't mean any offense!" Imogen knew from listening to the lower echelons of the entertainment industry —the third string makeup artists, the caterers, the production assistants—that most actors had major egos that needed constant reassurance. Praise and flattery were the expectation, no matter the level of actor. As the head of the A-list, Dolian Crawford had to boast the biggest head of them all. She would get farther with her questions if she patronized him a bit…not that she would have any trouble in that department.

"How about I start with my questions?" she asked to change the subject. Her companion watched with a bemused look as she withdrew a small, spiral notebook and pen from her purse. She opened it to her list of questions.

"Don't you want to record this? For clarity?" prompted Dolian.

Imogen flushed with embarrassment. It was her first celebrity interview and she undoubtedly looked like a fish floundering on the beach.

"Um…I didn't bring a recorder," she replied, her voice low and laced with shame.

He cocked his head to the side. "What happened to the phone I gave you?"

Following his train of thought, Imogen realized her new cell had a feature to record conversations, something her previous cell couldn't do after a particularly rough bang from Austin. She withdrew it from her purse and set it on the table, face up, before pressing the record button.

"Wait! The phone you gave me? I thought this came from the security guard who knocked my phone out of my hand."

Dolian nodded. "Yes, that's what I meant."

Having his attention solely on her, looking like a god descended directly from Mount Olympus, made Imogen feel flustered and awkward. For as many times as she had imagined this moment, both as a fantasy where they were on a romantic date and a dream for her blog that would catapult her into stardom, she had only ever envisioned herself to be as cool and mysterious as Dolian himself was known to be.

His gaze transfixed her, with an intensity that made her feel like the only person alive.

"Um…" Whether it was her nerves or simply the thin, mountain air, her voice sounded smaller. "You are a notoriously private person. Why did you decide to give an interview today?"

Dolian shrugged without looking at her. "I'm an actor. It's a part of the job."

"Don't you think you'd be better served giving an interview with a more established media outlet? Any number of journalists would give their right arm for an opportunity like this."

With an unbecoming snort of derision, Dolian shook his head. "Yes, I'm well aware that the vultures are lurking. While it may seem as though I'm…selective…in my choice of interviews, that's only because I want to ensure that I am represented in the most honest light possible. Not everyone is as committed to journalistic integrity as you, Imogen."

Now a blush burned across her cheeks for a different kind of embarrassment. No one had ever given her such high praise before.

"What do you know about my integrity, Mr. Crawford?"

He leaned forward, holding her eyes like a magnet. "It's Dolian. And I know more than you think." Settling back in his chair, he gestured towards her list of questions. "Now, let's focus on the real questions. Fire away."

FIVE

"I worked with the guy for four months straight, and even I can't tell you much about him!"
-*Cassandra Mage,* Agent Reckless *co-star*

And so it went for the next two hours. While he revealed more about his personality and preferences than Imogen ever encountered in any other article, Dolian ultimately revealed very little about his past or who he truly was as a person. Imogen discovered that he was not particularly funny; all of the comedy from his movies had merely been an ability to reflect the humor already written in the script. If anything, his boastful nature and need to impress her dampened her spirits considerably.

She also realized as they went through her list of questions that his responses changed depending on the nature of the question. For example, when talking about him as a person, Dolian reported that he was rather laidback and unassuming. Someone who always wanted to go with the flow to see where he wound up. Yet when they moved to start discussing his upcoming film, Dolian gave very striking details about his need for control, how the studio didn't set a strict enough filming schedule, so he ordered the director to abide by the schedule Dolian provided or the actor threatened to walk.

After a brief moment of reflection, Dolian asked her not to include that in her article.

She nodded along with every word, taking notes as quickly as her hand could write. The muscles in her fingers and wrist burned, but she didn't want to miss a thing. It was a good thing that he suggested she record the interview on her phone because there was no way she could have remembered everything. Even as her fingers cramped and her back grew stiff, Imogen hung on to his tales with eyes of rapture. This interview was every journalist's dream.

Everything about Dolian Crawford drew her in. The lithe way he moved, the casual style in which he dressed, his smile that on rare moments turned genuine enough to bring out his dimples—she could always tell the difference. His entire persona was breathtaking and if it weren't for the hot sun beating down on her so that sweat trickled down her spine, Imogen would continue to question if it was all a figment of her imagination.

After exhausting her list of questions and all the follow up questions his answers inspired, several hours had gone by. She would need to be leaving soon if she was going to make it home in time to pick up Austin.

"Wow, Mr. Crawford…this was absolutely fantastic!" Imogen gushed as she glanced through her notes. "I can't thank you enough."

He smiled at her. "Please call me Dolian. It would be nice to have someone who wasn't so formal around me."

Imogen's nose crinkled, which he immediately noted.

"What is it?"

"Well…" hedged Imogen, nervously chewing on her bottom lip. "It's just that you can be a little…intimidating."

Dolian's eyes widened in surprise. "I intimidate people?"

She nodded.

"Do I intimidate you, Imogen Reilly?"

It came out laced with innuendo, spoken in the kind of low, sensual tones reserved for lovers. Imogen's cheeks flushed as her schoolgirl crush reared its ugly head at being so addressed.

"Perhaps."

Something passed between them, something Imogen didn't know how to place or identify. But they held each other's gaze far longer than necessary, both too still in fear of breaking the spell. It wasn't until Huxley returned with a tray of light sandwiches that Imogen or Dolian could break their eyes away.

"Sir," was all Huxley said as he forcefully placed the tray on the table between them.

"God, I'm so sorry, Imogen!" Dolian cried. "I promised you lunch and then I babbled on so long that I forgot to make us something!"

She shrugged. "I'm happy you were able to answer all my questions. No harm done. I really should be going, though." Imogen began loading her purse with her notebook, pens, and phone.

"So soon?" he asked quietly.

Imogen laughed. "I've taken up enough of your time, Mr. Crawford, and you've been more than generous."

Dolian hurriedly got up and followed her back towards the house. "But I haven't given you a full tour of the house yet!" he objected.

That stopped Imogen in her tracks. She turned to him, eyebrows raised and mouth gaping. "You're willing to give me a tour of your *private residence*?"

For some reason, her answer seemed to help him relax. His shoulders dropped and the bright smile returned. "Of course, Imogen. I wouldn't invite you all the way here if I wasn't going to show you around."

"Could I maybe take a photo? To share with the article?" Imogen asked hopefully.

His forehead creased as he frowned at her question. Dolian glanced out towards the garden before replying, "I'll allow you to take a few photos of me, but not my home. I need it to remain private."

Her cheeks burned with shame. Of course he wanted to keep his property to himself! Look at how far he lived from others! Dolian Crawford, recluse extraordinaire, was generous enough to give an interview for the first time in his career, and Imogen had to keep pushing him for more. She was no better than Evette Coleman, leeching off a celebrity who was still a human being with a right to boundaries at the end of the day.

"I am so sorry, Mr. Crawford! That was completely out of line on my part! I shouldn't have even asked."

He shrugged, an offhand gesture of nonchalance meant to put her at ease. "I would have found it strange if you didn't. C'mon—we'll start in here."

Dolian led them through the hidden glass door panel, keeping Imogen firmly on his right, as far away from the pool as possible, and back down the dark hallway towards the foyer. Once again, all of the doors were shut, but Dolian could somehow tell them all apart, for he crossed to a door opposite them and took her inside a gorgeous home theater.

The room was designed to look like they entered outer space. It was pitch black, save for thousands of tiny pinpricks of light shining like stars on the ceiling, walls, and floors. Only after her eyes adjusted to the darkness could Imogen make out the thick leather recliners; three chairs deep in stadium style rows that ascended up towards what almost looked like a makeshift concessions counter. Even the projector hanging from the ceiling was black with the same minuscule lights.

"It probably sounds crazy, considering what I do for a living, but I love watching movies. All movies, from the golden age of Hollywood all the way to this year's new releases. I study them, as it were. There are so many great actors to learn from." Dolian spoke with reverence, looking about the room like it was his true pride and joy. Imogen had the sense that this was one of the first true statements he had made about himself all day.

"I love movies, too," she ventured. "That's why I wanted to be an entertainment journalist. Never fancied myself much of an actor, and I don't have enough patience to do any of the behind the scenes stuff. Writing about it just seemed like the closest thing."

Dolian nodded. "I can tell you have a passion for them like I do."

She cocked her head in surprise. "How do you know that?"

There was a pregnant pause before Dolian replied, almost abashedly, "I read through your blog in preparation for the interview."

Imogen gasped. "Oh my god, you DIDN'T."

He merely nodded, causing her to break out in a fit of giggles.

"Just remember—I'm still hitting my stride!" She laughed, equally stunned and mortified that he would read her blog articles that mostly consisted of gossip passed through four or more low-end workers from studio lots.

Dolian's returning smile was radiant. The more she giggled, the wider it became, like the sound pleased him.

"They were all wonderful," he insisted. "Let's continue! There's a lot more to see."

The tour continued through a state of the art home gym where all four walls were made of mirrors. Judging by the direction they turned to get there, Imogen suspected it was built into the very mountain itself. Next came an office that Dolian humbly stated was more to store his awards than anything. Imogen had to actively restrain herself from picking up one of his Academy Awards just to simply say she'd actually held one in her hands.

When they returned back into the circular foyer, Dolian errantly gestured towards one of the closed doors and said, "That leads down to Huxley's room and the security office. It's nothing special. I only ever go there if I need to make a phone call."

Imogen gave him the side eye, trying not to appear too

confused in case the answer seemed obvious. "Why would you need to go there to make a phone call?" she asked.

Dolian shrugged. "The security office is the only room where there's any kind of cell service or Wi-Fi," he commented before quickly changing directions. "That door will lead us to the stairs for the garage and gardens. Would you like to see the bedrooms?"

Imogen whirled to face him in surprise. "You're willing to show me your bedroom?"

Dolian's eyes widened. "Should I not? Is that inappropriate?"

She snorted in derision. "It's kind of inappropriate, but I'd still love to see it!"

Once again, the same hungry smile that didn't quite extend to his eyes lit his face, vanishing in an instant. Imogen minutely shook her head, certain she was seeing things. Her fiendish excitement was literally making her crazy.

He placed an arm in the small of her back and led them down the hallway back into the living area. This time they curved around the couches towards the staircase at the end of the kitchen, following it up to the balcony that hovered over the seating area.

"This first door is one of the bathrooms," he explained. "Nothing fancy. Here is a guest bedroom, here is a bigger guest bedroom, and this," Dolian gestured to the last door, "is my bedroom."

He swung open the door and waited for Imogen to enter first, cautiously watching as she stepped over the threshold. A second terrace had been carved out of the mountain, the double doors of which provided the only light in the room.

The walls almost looked painted, despite being the same stone texture as the rest of the rooms; a whitewash that lightened the space. A huge teakwood bed was centered in the room, with a built-in side table jutting from the headboard. Two closed doors occupied the wall behind it. A lone standing mirror leaned against the corner to Imogen's left.

It was so simple and minimal that Imogen almost felt let down. She had expected another breathtaking piece of architecture and design whereas this space looked and felt more like an afterthought. There wasn't even so much as a picture hanging on the wall.

Dolian came to stand beside her, his intense gaze focused on her face. "It's a bit plain, right?"

Her traitorous cheeks flushed again at how well he seemed to read her thoughts. "I'm sure it's a very relaxing place to sleep," Imogen offered lightly.

He chuckled. "I've kept it very simple on purpose, waiting for the day I can bring a wife here."

Now *that* piqued her interest.

"Oh?" she asked innocently. "Someone you're already dating?"

A casual shrug and a quick survey of the room. "Someone I've loved from afar. Just waiting for the opportune moment."

The words sent poor Imogen's heart into a tailspin and she tried hard to keep the tears from her eyes at this revelation. It wasn't like she actually believed she had a shot with Dolian Crawford, movie star of the century, but it was harder for the fantasy to exist if she had to see him with some gorgeous starlet on his arm. Jealousy wound around her heart like a snake.

"This is all incredible, Mr. Crawford," she managed to whisper. "Thank you so much for everything."

Imogen exited the room, hastily descending the stairs before any tears could betray her disappointment. To her utter amazement, Dolian Crawford followed her.

"But there's so much more to see!" he called over her shoulder.

They reached the foyer before he caught up to her, grabbing her shirt sleeve to stop her from leaving. Imogen stopped, taking a deep breath to calm her shattered heart, before turning around to face him.

"I'm so sorry, Mr. Crawford, but I really have to go. There's somebody waiting for me and I need to get to him."

Dolian's eyes blackened as his nostrils flared. "You double booked me? Me—Dolian Crawford?"

His change in demeanor was so abrupt and cold that Imogen staggered backward a step. "No, Mr. Crawford! Of course not! I just wasn't expecting to be here so long and now I have another commitment."

Imogen couldn't admit to him that she had to care for her baby brother. It would be mortifying to tell Dolian how pathetic her life truly was, let alone give him an indication of how poor her family lived. Shame firmly clamped her mouth shut.

"I see."

Dolian's back was now ramrod straight. He turned to a door, magically identifying which was the front, and opened it wide, glaring at her.

She wanted to crawl into a hole and die. Never had she been so embarrassed…and what's worse, Imogen wasn't entirely sure why. Their interview went well. He provided excellent material for her to write an exclusive exposé, but now she felt as if she was leaving with her tail between her legs.

"It was such an honor, Mr. Crawford," Imogen whispered as she passed him, keeping her eyes downcast and nodding to his indomitable form. Somehow the driver from before was already waiting next to the same sedan to take her home.

"I certainly hope your 'commitment' is worth it!" Dolian snapped before slamming the door shut.

It was such an unfair, cruel response that Imogen couldn't stop her tears from falling. Once again, the driver remained silent, closing the door behind her after she settled into the back seat. This trip made her grateful for the black partition so that she could wallow in her misery, privately.

SIX

Imogen barely made it in time to catch the last bus out to the day center. She would have to spend money on a taxi home, something that never went over well because Austin always got so excited over the prospect of riding in a vehicle that he became louder than usual, often upsetting the drivers. By the time she arrived at the day center, however, the sign on the door indicated they were closed.

And thanks to the long interview Imogen recorded on her phone at Dolian Crawford's house, it was dead.

Her heart sank as panic set in. She had no clue where Austin was, nor did she have the ability to find out. Desperate banging on the door did nothing; all the employees had already gone home for the day.

Having no choice but to go home and charge her phone, Imogen flagged down a cab and returned to their apartment.

To her surprise, the lights were on in the windows, and relief consumed her as she opened the door to find Austin on the couch coloring in one of the adult coloring books she bought him, only to find Sylvia sitting in one of the kitchen bistro chairs with her arms crossed and her face thunderous.

"Do you have any idea how much work I've missed?!" she screeched.

"Mom, I'm sorry. I got—" Imogen started to explain, but there was no way to talk her mother down on this one.

"YOU ARE THE ONE WHO WANTS HIM HERE!" Sylvia bellowed. "I have told you—repeatedly—that Austin needs to go into a group home! That you're not responsible enough to handle him! Thank God the day center had me down as his primary guardian or they probably would have called social services! How could you be so selfish, Imogen?!"

Tears spilled over as Imogen's vision blurred for the second time that day in burning shame. There really was no excuse. Austin should have been her top priority, but she got swept up in the thrill of the moment to have such amazing access to her favorite actor. It hardly seemed worth it at this point.

Sylvia stood up, pointing her finger in Imogen's face. "You are going to find a way to make up that money for me, Imogen! We can't afford for me to lose those hours! I don't care what you have to do, but this will never happen again, d'you hear me?!"

Her mother didn't wait for a response, merely swept from the room without saying goodbye to either of them. The door slammed shut behind her.

While she hated to have Sylvia so upset, Austin was the true victim here. Imogen promised to take care of him and then let him down after what had already been a bad morning. Now, without Dolian's breathtaking smile and handsome face before her, getting a tour of his home seemed like the dumbest reason to disappoint her brother. She sat down next to him on the lumpy sofa and wrapped her arms around his shoulders.

"I'm so sorry, buddy!" Imogen cried. "I should have come back for you on time!"

Austin patted her arm and leaned his head so that it rested on top of Imogen's. It was as close to accepting an apology as he could express. But the sheer power of his love and forgiveness brought fresh tears to Imogen's eyes.

"We'll spend the whole day together tomorrow, I promise," she vowed. "You're the most important person in my life, Austin."

He turned and smiled at her, pointing to his chest as if asking, "Me? Really?"

She nodded. "I love you, bud! Can I make you something to eat!"

Austin bounced on the seat and repeatedly made the N sound, which Imogen knew was his way of requesting nuggets. In one of his more child-like endearments, Austin loved dinosaur shaped chicken nuggets more than any other food.

Imogen let out a watery laugh. "Yep, I'll make some dino nuggies! Coming right up!"

It was a simple enough task that allowed her mind to wander as muscle memory allowed her to make dinner without much forethought. She felt awful for leaving Austin at the day center like that, and for making her mother go to pick him up. Losing hours at work was something they simply couldn't afford for Sylvia to do, but maybe if she could get her article posted right away, some hefty endorsements would start as her blog took off.

Except Imogen no longer felt comfortable even writing about Dolian Crawford. Their interaction ended on such a sour note that it spoiled the entire day for her, despite the fact that she knew she would dream of his impressive home for months. She wasn't sure what disappointed her more— the fact that he acted so angry and cold when Imogen left or that meeting him in real life had been nothing like her fantasies for the past eight years. It was a bitter pill to swallow.

Once Austin was happily settled in with chicken nuggets, fruit, and potato chips in front of his favorite cartoons, Imogen pulled out her archaic laptop and sat down at the tiny kitchen table to write. The computer had been part of a school grant to fund technology in classrooms, but like most nice things in Compton, all of them had been sold off as soon as they were passed out to students. Imogen bought it from it's third owner for only $50 and had her neighbor jailbreak it for her to bypass all the school login requirements. Now it only worked if it was plugged in, and there was a corner of the screen that was entirely blacked out, but Imogen knew asking her mom for a new computer would have been akin to asking for a roundtrip ticket to Paris.

Writing had always been the one school subject at which Imogen excelled. She never particularly cared about school, having no desire or ability to go to college, and since Austin always needed so much help at home, her homework wasn't high on her priority list. It had therefore surprised her in junior high when her English teacher invited her to join the student paper. But after seeing her name in print for her very first article (a scathing indictment on the food vendor in the cafeteria), Imogen was hooked. She wrote for the student paper all through junior high and high school, eventually becoming the entertainment editor her senior year. She even won an award at the county competition for student papers.

Everything she told Dolian had been true; Imogen was as fascinated and intrigued by Hollywood as he claimed to be. Watching movies was her favorite past time, especially because it was an activity that always kept Austin's attention. It made both of them happy to curl up on the couch or the bed and watch something together. Since she couldn't act, had no talent with makeup, computer effects, or building things, and couldn't manage a studio lot schedule, writing about movies and their stars really was the perfect fit for her.

And she had tried, in vain, for years to get a job with a real news show. They all wanted college degrees and "connections," which Imogen learned meant the hiring managers looked for nepotism or sex. Imogen offered neither.

Still, it hadn't been all bad to start her blog and find her own stories. Since they didn't have the space for her to have any sort of visual setup to use as an influencer in the apartment, Imogen primarily shared photos of herself at more notable locations around L.A. Austin would happily sit beside her as long as she provided him with a snack and something to do, like a coloring book or a word search puzzle. And now that he was enrolled in the day center, she hoped it would provide more opportunities for her to chase a lead.

Assuming she hadn't burned a bridge with their staff. She

grabbed a Post It note and wrote down a reminder to call them the next day to ask.

For once, the blank document sat open in front of her and the words wouldn't come. Her fingers were poised over the keys, ready to crank out an article on two time Academy Award winning movie star Dolian Crawford...and crickets. She couldn't reconcile the man she believed him to be with the boastful, chameleon-like persona he presented. There was very little in her notes that indicated a real person; his words were chosen with care to project the man he wanted people to believe him to be.

Her eyes lit up as Imogen realized that was her angle. As much as she obsessed over him, another worshipful report about how "wonderful" Dolian Crawford was wouldn't rock the entertainment world. No, she needed to be bold. To call him out for his true nature, letting fans gain some true insight on their beloved idol.

The creative juices started flowing as she typed out words as fast as her fingers would allow.

Dolian Crawford-Unmasked

After a lackluster experience at the Agent Reckless *premiere, none other than yours truly received the world's most coveted invitation: an exclusive interview with Mr. Hollywood himself, Dolian Crawford! Let's not kid ourselves—this was a dream come true for any journalist worth their salt. I would have been a fool to turn down the opportunity. However, when they say never meet your heroes, there's a reason why.*

The 29 year old Love From Verona *star was gracious enough to open his home to me. Nestled into the California hills, the actor's gothic mansion is built right into the rock bed itself. Featuring an indoor pool, movie theater, and industrial home gym, the castle includes four bedrooms and five bathrooms. And ladies, there's a state of the art security system, so don't even try it!*

Although Dolian denied the use of photography during the private tour, he revealed more about his character than any other reporter has seen before, including that he loves to cook his own meals and grows his own food. And while that might make your little eco-friendly heart swoon, Dolian disclosed the true reason is overwrought paranoia about grocery shopping. Indeed, with the location being so remote that there was no cellular service (the horror!), one could only imagine the nightmare involved with deliveries.

We spent the better part of the afternoon exploring his spacious abode because the heartthrob would leave no stone unturned. LITERALLY.

The only thing bigger than Dolian's home is his ego. Apparently the two time Oscar winner needs flattery more than oxygen, and I couldn't supply enough of it.

While I have yet to see Agent Reckless, I have peeled back another layer on the reclusive Dolian Crawford persona, and I have to say—I find him to be rather lacking.

It was close to one in the morning, with Austin long since asleep on the couch, before Imogen finally clicked "Publish" on her blog. Just for good measure, she sent out a newsletter to her 1,100 followers about her inside scoop on a Hollywood A-lister. While that might not be enough to garner much traction initially, it was all Imogen could do for the moment. She would have to reach out to the Contact tomorrow.

The very thought made her nose wrinkle in disgust as she finally laid down to sleep.

SEVEN

"Dolian Crawford can write his ticket in Hollywood. Every woman wants to date him and every man wants to be him."
-Cosmopolitan Magazine

Just as Imogen suspected, the Contact responded instantly the next morning, texting that they would meet in their usual spot in Beverly Hills that afternoon. Dread filled her stomach. She couldn't even bring herself to eat a slice of toast with Austin.

Too distraught at what the afternoon would entail, Imogen didn't bother picking up her phone again. She gave Austin her sole attention, coloring and helping him work through some of his flash cards to improve his speech. He had occupational therapy that afternoon, which gave her the perfect reason to be out and about so that she avoided another fight with Sylvia.

Avoidance seemed to be the option both Imogen and

Sylvia chose as they kept their eyes downcast and stayed in separate rooms during the brief span of time her mom came home. After a two hour nap, Sylvia changed her clothes and went downstairs to work a shift at the convenience store on the ground floor of the building. The tension in the apartment only amplified after she left, however, as guilt set in. Imogen hated fighting with her mom, especially over Austin.

I'm a horrible daughter as well as a terrible sister, she thought miserably.

At one o'clock, Imogen held firmly to Austin's hand as they walked down to the bus stop. His occupational therapist wasn't far from the bus line, and the sun beat down on them as they ambled down the block. Austin was in good spirits, keeping up with Imogen's quick pace better than normal. She had to hurry if she was going to meet the Contact on time.

The Contact was a secret Imogen kept from everyone. A good journalist never revealed their sources, but in Imogen's case, she couldn't reveal someone she had technically never met.

When Imogen first decided to write her blog, she had no idea how to make contact with anyone who was part of Hollywood. All of the studios denied her request for interviews, and when she tried to get a visitor's pass to meet people, she wasn't allowed in any areas that had worthwhile connections. On a whim, she decided to try sitting in a bar at a hotel in Beverly Hills, a swanky spot called The Majestic, that was often used for press junkets.

Since her clothing stuck out like a neon sign, Imogen had tucked herself into the last barstool in the corner, something almost completely obscured by a potted Ficus tree. It allowed her to overhear some of the gossip from the patrons drinking at the bar and sitting in the booth behind her without garnering much notice.

When she was just about to leave after not securing any juicy leads for *Hollywood Unmasked,* a payphone on the wall began to ring. After several shrill chimes, no one made a move to answer it, so Imogen plucked the phone off the hook herself.

"H-hello?" she had mumbled.

"Good afternoon," a lush, deep voice had purred. "Do you always answer calls from strangers?"

Imogen swallowed thickly. "I do when I'm desperate," she sighed. "Who is this?"

"Just a contact. Someone and no one, whichever you need me to be."

"Did you mean to call me?" Imogen said in a squeak. The man sounded like a Batman villain.

"Maybe. Do you need someone to talk to?"

She snorted. "I need more than that kind of help."

"I may be able to help," the voice replied. "The desperate ones always need the most help."

Even then, Imogen had felt skeptical. "What's the price? No one does anything for free for someone they don't know."

The voice had chuckled, a rich, throaty sound that made Imogen's heart rate spike. "A favor to be collected at another time. Now, what makes you desperate?"

"I-I need to find a contact in the movie biz...someone who's connected to Hollywood enough that they'll help me find the stories worth writing about," Imogen sniffled. Tears pooled at the corners of her eyes as she processed just how desperate she felt. If she didn't make any headway soon, her mother would have to find someone else to care for Austin and Imogen couldn't stomach the thought.

To her surprise, the voice laughed again, though it was much colder than before. "I can certainly help you with that!"

"You can?" It seemed too good to be true, like the serpent offering the apple to Eve.

"I'm a man of my word," he promised. "Now, what shall I call you?"

"Glenda," Imogen replied without thinking. There was no way she was going to give him her real name.

Another chuckle told her the voice recognized her lie. "Very well, *Glenda*. Be sure to keep an eye out for falling houses. I'll call you on this phone next week, Tuesday. Answer at precisely three o'clock."

"Yes, sir," Imogen whispered.

"Oh, and Glenda?" the voice asked sternly.

"Yes?"

"Tell no one about this call. Ever. The repercussions would be deadly."

And the line cut, the blaring tone in her ear making Imogen jump.

That had been four years ago. As the Contact's information proved to be more and more legitimate, she had come to rely on him for everything, from advice to reassurance. It had only been within the past two years Imogen had provided her cell phone, but with every text, he reminded her that she could not tell a soul of their exchange. The threats became less and less veiled. Over the past few months, the Contact had hinted at cashing in his so-called "favor." Imogen couldn't even fathom what it might be.

Every time she texted him, a loathing so strong and tangible crept across her skin like a spider. While his information might have been useful, it certainly never supplied enough of an inside scoop to constitute risking her life. Imogen was only able to track down certain makeup artists and warehouse craftsman on the bigger films thanks to the Contact's tips, and yet it irked her that she relied on him so. After all the time that passed, she was really no further along in the entertainment industry as she had been when she first picked up the phone. She relied on the Contact in a way that she didn't rely on anyone else. It was unnerving, and to Imogen, felt very much like failure and vulnerability.

For some reason, he always insisted their "meetings" take place with the same payphone at The Majestic. When she tried calling the number the Contact used to text her, a computer voice stated that it wasn't a real number and the call couldn't be completed. Imogen didn't know what to make of that and felt it wasn't appropriate to ask a man who repeatedly threatened death if you revealed his conversation.

Presently, Imogen scrambled into the bar at the hotel where the payphone was already ringing. More than one person glared at her, though she couldn't decide if it was her behavior or her black biker shorts and permanently stained t-shirt from a high school dance that was most offensive. She was breathless when she picked up the phone and whispered, "Yes?"

"You're late." The reprimand in the Contact's voice was cold and cruel.

"The bus had to help a disabled person," Imogen replied. She just left out the part that the disabled person was her brother, who was suddenly fascinated with the crank to open the bus doors. Austin made the driver open and close the doors for him multiple times before Imogen could drag him out.

"You're also going viral."

"Really?!" Imogen still hadn't checked her phone since traveling anywhere with Austin usually meant he needed her full attention. He had wandered off to inspect something or someone more than once. Those with Down Syndrome were known for their impulsivity, and her brother was no exception.

She whipped her phone out now from the canvas tote hanging over her shoulder. The screen instantly lit up with dozens of notifications. A quick glance told her most of them were negative. People were accusing her of lying. The few comments previewed called her horrible names and issued death threats.

"Oh my god!" Imogen whimpered.

The Contact tsked. "You should have known better than to attack Dolian Crawford."

"I didn't *attack* him!" she argued. "There was nothing like that in the article!"

"Semantics." His sigh sounded heavy, as if even the Contact hated what he was about to say. "You need to issue a retraction."

"What?! Why?" Imogen continued to scroll through the numerous responses on her blog post. Millions of people now followed her, and it had been shared over fifty thousand times. Her email inbox was flooded with requests from major news companies requesting a response.

"Because, Glenda, this kind of press is *not* what you need, nor what you can tolerate! Nor is it an accurate representation of Dolian Crawford, who—need I remind you—is the world's media darling."

Imogen bristled, incensed that the proposed solution was to snuff her opinion simply because it contradicted with the general public's. "You don't know that it's inaccurate."

"Yes, I do." The finality in his tone conveyed that he was not willing to discuss the topic any further.

"I'm...." she hesitated to reveal the truth to him, especially given the circumstances around her article. "I'm scared right now."

"As you should be. You shattered the perfect image of the industry's most beloved member."

"No, not for that." Imogen shook her head. Dropping her voice to barely above a whisper in case anyone who was within earshot overheard, she explained, "Two of the people I encountered at the movie premiere were reported dead the next morning."

"People die every day, Glenda," the Contact pointed out. It sounded like he exhaled from a cigarette.

"But these were both people who had bad interactions with me *on the night they were murdered.*" Imogen cupped her hand around the mouthpiece of the phone as she admitted the last part. "What if I'm implicated?"

There was a very long pause before the Contact answered. "Did you have anything to do with their deaths?"

She rolled her eyes impatiently. "Of course not!" Imogen snapped.

"Then what does it matter if you're implicated?"

"There are people I love that I need to protect!" She

instantly visualized her brother, knowing her mother would use a police investigation as a reason to force Austin into a group home, away from Imogen.

"What do you know of love, Glenda? Love is for adults, not children like yourself!" the Contact snarled angrily. It was the most visceral reaction she'd ever heard from him.

Imogen's jaw clenched. This was definitely the wrong time to state that she knew what love was, thanks to her love for Dolian Crawford. Instead, she ground out, "I have to go."

"You've made a royal mess of things," the Contact accused unsympathetically.

"That's all you've got for me?" she cried helplessly, throwing her free hand up in frustration. "Can't you tell me anything useful?"

"I did. Retract your article. Ignore whatever tabloid fodder you're reading about the movie premiere."

All of the fight went out of her, just like it always did. In the end, Imogen was always too afraid to rock the boat, take risks, or ever stand up for herself. It was what made her a doormat to her mother and a lackluster journalist. "The article's already been shared thousands of times. Retracting it won't do anything."

His words were bitter and unmoving. "You made your bed. Lie in it. Maybe next time you'll come to me first."

Tears pricked at the corner of her eyes as she angrily dabbled at them with the hem of her t-shirt. "Gee, thanks. Anything else?"

The Contact sighed. "Just remember, Evette Coleman and Jesse Ramirez's deaths were not your fault. Making nice with Dolian Crawford is the only thing that matters." The dial tone sounded in her ears as the line went dead.

It wasn't until Imogen stepped out onto the sunny street in front of The Majestic that she realized she never identified Evette Coleman or Jesse Ramirez as the murder victims.

EIGHT

"Things like this just don't happen to people like me!"
-Make-A-Wish recipient, Adyson Kyle, with Dolian Crawford

Speaking to the Contact made Imogen feel worse than ever. She couldn't stop scrolling through comments where she was labeled a "whore," "cunt," and "worse than a parasite desperately clinging for a minute of fame." That one hurt a little more since the person put more thought into it before commenting. Everyone on the internet imagined her to be a liar, citing all of the numerous ways in which they believed Dolian Crawford to be a charming, lovable idol.

Except none of them had concrete examples, Imogen rationalized as she read comment after vicious comment. The closest any of them came was the mother of a Make-A-Wish recipient who spent time on set during a film Dolian shot two years ago in Vancouver. She issued a statement that the Dolian Crawford her daughter got to meet before passing away brought a smile to her daughter's face that their family would always treasure.

And while Imogen had no doubt that was true, who had it in their hearts to be cruel to a dying child? That hardly proved Dolian Crawford wasn't obsessed with flattery and praise like every other actor.

Still, her blog had done what she wanted it to do. Imogen Reilly was now a household name across the hills of Hollywood. The attention was primarily negative as far as fan reactions, which was to be expected, but it did mean that people were finally reading her articles. Views skyrocketed on all of her previous pieces, and as Imogen gleefully checked her email, several sponsors had reached out to her to broker deals with ad placements on her blog. It was like winning the lottery jackpot—all Imogen could see were dollar signs.

Simultaneously wanting a pick-me-up and to celebrate the money that would soon roll in, Imogen headed across the street to one of the trendier coffee shops in Beverly Hills. She often took her laptop there to work in the corner since so many celebrities and their assistants frequented the area. While it never led to much gossip-wise, Imogen enjoyed many a quiet thrill to turn and find the likes of Reese Witherspoon or Theo James behind her.

Today, however, entering the busy caffeine hub felt like stepping into the spotlight. Everyone seemed to be looking at her, pointing and whispering to their companions as if they couldn't believe Imogen was real. While she didn't feature many photographs on *Hollywood Unmasked*, there were enough so that any reasonable person would know what she looked like. The scrutiny felt awful, and Imogen hastily pulled a pair of oversized sunglasses out of her bag to try and cover her face.

After splurging on a Frappuccino (what did calories matter when one was on the brink of breakdown?) under the name *Glenda*, Imogen tucked herself into a corner next to a trash can, rubbing her fingers along her temple. It succeeded in nursing her growing headache as well as shielding more of her face from the prying eyes of coffee patrons. Perhaps if she reverted back to the days of her childhood, whereby not seeing them meant they couldn't see her, it would make Imogen forget their judgmental scorn.

She dashed forward when her drink was called, turning abruptly on her heel, only to crash into a hard chest. Two strong hands reached out to grab her biceps and prevent her from falling over. Imogen's heart sank when she looked up to thank her rescuer only to find none other than Dolian Crawford standing before her.

"Imogen," he said smoothly, his gravelly voice like silk and honey. "We meet again."

Not once in all the years she had frequented this establishment, had Imogen ever seen Dolian inside. To her knowledge, water was his drink of choice. He had even once been quoted in a rare tv appearance as one of the few people on the planet who despised caffeinated drinks of any kind as a stimulant. "There's just something off about the taste to me," a smoldering Dolian had crooned to Kelly Ripa.

Now, as his warm hands still kept her upright, Imogen felt faint. Her mouth hung agape as she stumbled to remember how to form coherent words. The lid of her drink had popped off on impact, and there was whipped cream and chocolate flakes on the actor's tailored blazer. What were the odds that not only would he show up in a coffee house on the very day her article about him went viral, but that she would walk into him in an epic showdown that more than one coffee patron blatantly filmed with their phones?

"Sir, can you please replace this drink?" Dolian asked one of the baristas over her shoulder. "Add it to my tab."

Dolian's face returned to hers, his eyes a swirling storm of emotions that Imogen couldn't read. She wanted a black hole to swallow her on the spot.

"I'm so sorry, Mr. Crawford!" Imogen finally gushed. "I'll pay for the dry cleaning, I swear!" It would probably cost more than her family's rent for the next three months, but she would take out a loan if it meant making things right.

He offered her a tight smile. "For this old thing? It's hardly worth the trouble. I never liked it much anyway." He gestured to the blazer that easily had to be a custom piece worth thousands of dollars.

A few young women watching started to cheer as Dolian slipped off the blazer to reveal a form fitting black t-shirt underneath. Even his rippling ab muscles were visible through the fabric.

He flashed a quick smile towards them, causing more cheers, before stepping around her to accept Imogen's new drink on her behalf. "Come," ordered Dolian. "We have some things to discuss."

Her muscles moved on autopilot as she allowed him to lead her through the throng of cell phones and peering faces. Once again, his hand was sealed around her waist in a way that suggested far more familiarity than anyone ever achieved with the megastar. The same black BMW with the Asian driver had somehow managed to procure a spot directly in front of the coffeehouse. He held open the back door of the vehicle for them as Dolian and Imogen approached.

She stopped short, her breathing bordering on hyperventilating as she processed what was happening. "Mr. Crawford, I am so sorry about your blazer. I swear on my life that I will replace it or dry clean it—whichever you prefer! But I can't get in that car with you."

"Oh? And why is that?" Dolian whipped the perfect pair of Aviator sunglasses out of the pocket in his jeans. Settled onto his face, they made him look every inch the King of Hollywood.

Imogen swallowed thickly. "Because of the article I wrote."

"Dolian! Dolian!" A mob consisting of paparazzi and teenage girls suddenly swarmed them on both sides. The chauffeur stepped forward immediately to usher the two of them inside. It was a frenzy, with bright flashes blinding Imogen and lots of shouting. She didn't think as she dove into the waiting backseat of the BMW, with Dolian close behind. The flashes continued after the door closed, with hands and faces pressed against the glass.

"Are you two dating, Dolian?"

"Is this the same blogger who wrote about you?"

"Dolian, take me instead!"

"We love you, Dolian!"

It was pandemonium as the vehicle was suddenly surrounded on all sides with so many people that the driver could barely open the door enough to slip inside. The partition was down this time, and Imogen recognized Huxley in the passenger seat.

"Everything alright, sir?" he asked.

Dolian nodded. "Yes, right on time. Thank you, Huxley." He pressed a button on the door and the partition rose between the seats again. The chauffeur blared the car horn for a minute straight before people finally moved, allowing the car to steer into traffic.

It wasn't until all of the paparazzi were out of sight that Imogen finally allowed herself to breathe. Her hands were clammy with sweat and her heart threatened to beat through her ribcage. "Is it always like that?"

The actor snorted derisively. "It is when you're Dolian Crawford," he replied sarcastically. Imogen wasn't used to the harsh edge in his voice, and she involuntarily shivered.

"Please, just drop me off by the bus line," she pleaded. "I'll do whatever you want about the blazer. And the article," she added weakly. They both knew there was nothing she could do now about the article. The damage was done.

"I'm not taking you to a county bus," Dolian sneered. "Is that your usual method of transportation?"

Imogen's shoulders slumped and she couldn't look at him as she admitted the truth. "We can't afford a car. I never even got my driver's license." She remained hyper focused on her sneakers' laces as she awaited his response.

After a long moment, Dolian released a heavy sigh. "I would like to discuss your blog with you, if you don't mind."

She nodded glumly, eyes still trained on her shoes. "Yes, we can schedule a time to do that."

"I have already had to take the past couple days off from filming for you, Imogen," chided Dolian. "I would much rather talk now while I have you in front of me."

For you, Imogen.

Those words sent goosebumps skittering along her flesh.

Suddenly the backseat was too cold and too hot all at once. Her favorite movie star took a break out of his hectic schedule...*for her*.

Imogen didn't know what to make of this revelation.

She glanced down at her phone, realizing belatedly that she needed to pick Austin up in twenty minutes. Even if she caught the bus, she wouldn't make it in time. And after how badly Sylvia exploded last night over picking Austin up, there was no way Imogen would let that happen again today.

"Actually, I need to go pick up my brother," Imogen said. "If I can just pick him up and get him to the Day Center, I should have about an hour to speak with you before they close."

"The Day Center?" Dolian asked.

Imogen knew she needed to be honest. It was the least she could do after how well Dolian seemed to be taking the ruined jacket and bad press. "It's for adults with Down Syndrome. Adults like my brother, Austin. That's why I had to leave yesterday. I take care of him."

To her surprise, Dolian's features relaxed and his blue eyes grew warm as he regarded her. "That was your prior commitment?" he clarified.

Imogen nodded. "The Day Center is only open for certain hours, so if I need to do an interview or take photos for the blog, I have to do everything while they're open. Austin is at occupational therapy right now, though, so if I can make it in time to pick him up and get him there, I'm happy to discuss the article with you."

Dolian settled back into his seat, gently rubbing his index finger over his bottom lip as he regarded her. His Aviator sunglasses hung from the collar of his shirt, and in that moment he looked so rugged and sexy that Imogen had to bite back a moan. If only fifteen year old Imogen could see her now!

"No," he finally decided.

"No?" she repeated, confused.

"No," Dolian confirmed. "We are going to pick Austin up and I am going to treat you to dinner. Mexican food is your favorite, right? I know just the place. Huxley!" he called out as he hit the button to lower the partition. "Please book my usual table at Padre's. I'll have two guests with me this evening. What's the address so we can pick up your brother?" Dolian's face was angelic as he waited for Imogen's reply.

Her crush increased tenfold.

Yet, as she rattled off the address to Austin's occupational therapist, she couldn't help but wonder, when did she ever have a chance to tell Dolian Crawford, the world's biggest movie star, that Mexican was her favorite food?

NINE

Padre's turned out to be the best Mexican food Imogen ever tasted. Situated right on the ocean, the restaurant offered diners a sprawling view of the West coast unblemished with tourists as the beach was privately owned by the restaurant. A hostess with half her face painted into a skeleton, reminiscent of Dia de los Muertos, led them to a room separated with heavy tapestries that opened directly onto a balcony jutting out towards the ocean. She produced several large dry erase boards with a colorful array of markers for Austin to use, then later brought an easel out for convenience as he attempted to draw more. Artwork of any kind had always been a favorite past time for Austin since his therapists rewarded him with coloring sheets, new markers, and drawing paper whenever he worked hard during sessions.

With Austin happily occupied, the meal had been a dream come true for Imogen. Dolian ordered for the table and they ate family style, assembling whatever their own version of fajitas and tacos looked like. After Austin spit out every version of a taco she made, Imogen had been near to tears with embarrassment, explaining Austin preferred blander tastes, like chicken tenders or macaroni and cheese. Dolian summoned the waitress again to whisper something in her ear and only minutes later, a wide assortment of Austin's favorite foods arrived on a tray. Austin gleefully clapped, pointing triumphantly at the spread and yelling, "Good! Good!" He returned to his coloring easel with a small plate of food balanced on his lap, happy to color and eat at leisure.

Imogen didn't even want to imagine what the meal cost. For a restaurant to have such a prime location along with a secluded room specifically for guests like Dolian, she could only guess their bill would be somewhere in the five to six figure range.

It was the happiest she ever felt, and even the memory of the paparazzi surrounding their car or the terrible fallout that awaited her from the *Hollywood Unmasked* blog couldn't bring Imogen down from the high. She wanted to bask in the moment forever as the object of her infatuation continued to supply her with tortilla chips and queso while the setting sun set their skin aglow in the light. Austin was rarely this care-free, which was exactly the way she always wanted him to feel.

Dolian and Imogen chatted about errant things like their favorite movies, favorite actors, and different styles of cinema. It turned out they had far more in common than Imogen realized. Her girlish fantasies squealed with delight as the conversation flowed easily over such topics. This was what she always imagined a date with Dolian to be like.

Without realizing it, Dolian revealed far more of himself through the course of their conversation. Imogen surmised that he had been raised right there in Los Angeles County, likely from rougher beginnings, like herself. He didn't have any family members around anymore. For some reason that fact sounded off to Imogen, triggering a warning bell, as she tried to follow his conversation, running through Dolian Crawford factoids in her head. She wanted to double check her scrapbook of all things Dolian when she got home.

"So," she finally said, leaning forward on her elbows as she crossed her arms on the table. "I have to thank you for such a wonderful evening, but it definitely wasn't deserved. I should be the one treating you to something special."

He waved a hand airily. "This is nothing. Pedro is one of the few proprietors in L.A. that offers total privacy and discretion for his guests. It's one of my favorite places to eat. But yes, I would like to clear the air about your article."

She nodded. "I'm so sorry, Mr. Crawford. Our interview ended on such a strange note, and it made me feel awful to disappoint you. I never should have written an article out of anger."

Dolian smirked. "I can't forgive you if you don't start calling me 'Dolian.' And for the record, our interview didn't end well because I am a bit of a jealous beast. I shouldn't have assumed a commitment of any kind meant a romantic relationship." He nodded towards Austin. "It's natural for your brother to come first."

Either the waves were crashing louder than before or

there was a roaring sound in her ears. Did he just admit that he was *jealous* over the idea of Imogen dating someone?

"I'm not sure what to say," she admitted in a whisper.

"Say that you're single. That you feel this, too." There was a hunger in his gaze that made Imogen tremble. It was the same intensity that made her pause in the foyer of Dolian's house. There was something off about the feeling. Rather than giving her butterflies of delight, her stomach contained a can of worms. It was shocking, really, how often those two feelings could be misinterpreted as one another.

She bit down on her lip, contemplating her answer. "I *am* single. But I don't know what I feel right now. You're intimidating, remember?"

They shared a quick laugh at the inside joke. Later, when she tried to quiet her mind enough to go to sleep, Imogen knew the fact that she had an inside joke with the world's biggest star would make her giddy.

"Please say you'll give me a chance," Dolian begged. "I've been waiting for this for so long…" His voice trailed off as he leaned in closer. She leaned closer, too. Their faces were barely an inch apart, their noses on the verge of brushing against one another.

"Waiting for me?" she murmured, eyes wide and heart pounding.

"Yes," he breathed. Strong lips found hers on the exhale. It took several seconds for her brain to recalibrate from the short circuit lightning bolt that struck. She, Imogen Reilly, was kissing *the* Dolian Crawford!

Austin's loud clapping and grunts made Imogen jump like the edge of a white hot poker touched her skin. He pointed animatedly out to the water where a speedboat zoomed by, turning back to them to see if they found as much excitement in the discovery as he did. For a brief moment, Imogen felt grateful that Austin's speech wasn't better because there was no way he could tell Sylvia about the kiss. Guilt drowned the gratitude, however. What kind of terrible person feels thankful that their brother can't speak? That was a new low for Imogen.

"Thank you, Dolian," Imogen said, "but we really must be getting home. It's late."

Using his name was the only reason he didn't protest, she was sure of it. His posture stiffened again like it had the last time she needed to leave, but he quickly cracked both sides of his neck and his shoulders relaxed. "Of course," replied Dolian. "I'll let the driver know."

"What about Evette Coleman?" Imogen asked a few minutes later as they walked towards the car through a private exit.

He turned towards her sharply. "What about Evette Coleman?" Anger decorated his face, accentuating his powerful jawline.

Imogen was surprised at the emotion in his reaction and stopped abruptly to stare at him. "Remember? Police said she was murdered after attending your movie premiere?"

Was it a trick of the light or did his eyes darken at the reminder of the reporter's untimely death? It certainly wasn't her imagination that Dolian's nostrils flared or that his hands squeezed into fists at his sides.

"The important thing is that she's no longer bothering you," Dolian suggested after a moment. "Let it go. Please," he tacked on as a peace offering. He wrapped his right arm around her waist again, allowing his hand to fall lower on her hip this time than before. The move felt possessive, calculated, almost like a preventative measure in case she decided to run.

But there was no way Imogen could run away from something like this. All her dreams were coming to fruition. Not only had her entertainment gossip blog allowed her to meet Dolian Crawford, she had somehow managed to capture his attention. He took her out to dinner, including Austin, too, and then kissed her. A kiss that shook Imogen down to her core. This was the best day of her life.

So why did she have to force the smile on her face?

TEN

"It's not very often you have a co-star who is as generous with his craft as Dolian Crawford."
-Oscar winner, Paul Rudemyer

It took over twenty minutes of arguing before Dolian—begrudgingly—agreed to take Austin and Imogen to a bus stop. She couldn't think of anything more mortifying than having someone like Dolian Crawford in her neighborhood. It didn't matter that he alluded to humble beginnings like hers; he lived on a completely different plane than her now.

Her brother fell asleep on her shoulder on the bus ride home, giving Imogen a chance to check her phone again. A decision she immediately regretted as she saw the new headlines plastered on all the media outlets.

DOLIAN CRAWFORD SEEN WITH GOSSIP BLOGGER

A COFFEE DATE OR A COFFEE EXECUTION?

THE GOLD DIGGER STRIKES AGAIN

She groaned aloud. They were all accompanied by photographs of her with Dolian in front of the coffee shop at an angle where it looked like they could have been having a confrontation. Imogen didn't remember her body language to be so angry, but in the heat of that moment, anything could have been possible. Photographs certainly made the two of them look far more familiar with one another than they actually were. And the worst part was that every single article reported that they got into a black sedan together and drove off.

Mexican food never burned quite as much as when it came back up, and Imogen had a strong suspicion she was about to find out.

They only barely made it off the bus in time for Imogen to spew her guts on the sidewalk. Austin, thankfully, thumped her back while she puked, at least recognizing that her behavior meant something was wrong. She didn't want to search for him with vomit down her front.

The one thing Imogen hadn't counted on was Sylvia's presence inside their apartment. Fire lit her mother's eyes as she glared at her daughter, who wreaked of stomach acid. Austin shuffled off to his room after thumping Imogen once more on the back. In comfort or in solidarity, she didn't know.

"Where the hell have you been?" Sylvia hissed through clenched teeth. "I came home to a dark apartment, no dinner, and then you never answered any of my texts or calls!"

"I'm sorry, Mom, I haven't been checking my phone much today," Imogen replied weakly.

Sylvia grabbed her own cell phone off the kitchen counter and held it up at arm's length to show Imogen the screen. "No wonder since you're on the front page of every tabloid in the world right now!"

Imogen winced at the fury laced in the accusation. She didn't even bother reading the headline her mom showed her, already knowing it would be just as bad as the others. "I tried to explain to you about yesterday—"

Her mother cut her off with a wave of her hand. "Don't you dare make this out to be MY fault, Imogen! You had plenty of opportunities to warn me that you were meeting with that fake bozo all over our bedroom walls! That's the kind of important thing daughters tell their mothers!"

Rather than rise to meet her mother's tirade, Imogen sighed and walked down the hall towards their bedroom. If they were going to argue, the least she could do was get a clean t-shirt on and brush her teeth. Sylvia followed.

"Do you have any idea the impact all of this has had on me, huh?" her mother yelled. "All of my bosses saw! One of them even asked if this meant I would quit now that my daughter's rich boyfriend could support me! Are you dating this man, Imogen? Really?"

The screaming was too loud for Imogen's throbbing head. She still hadn't wrapped her mind around the day's events let alone thought of a reasonable explanation for her mother. Sylvia wanted a black and white answer to a question that was distinctly technicolored. One kiss over dinner did not a relationship make.

But that didn't mean Imogen was in denial that there was something different between Dolian and herself. He had never dated *anyone* to her knowledge, and she had been following his career since the early days. An evil voice in her subconscious started to question her information, though. Maybe he had dated other people. Padre's certainly seemed to offer the perfect amount of secrecy and discretion; there might be locations like that all over Los Angeles. It wasn't like Imogen had his direct phone number to ask him.

Although, Imogen did have someone's phone number. She never erased the initial text chain from the night she got her phone. The number likely belonged to Huxley since he was the keeper of secrets in Dolian Crawford's life, but she could always see if he could give her a direct number to his boss.

She ignored her mother's shouted diatribe as she pulled her phone from her pocket only to have the text preview on screen give her another near panic attack. The Contact was clearly infuriated with her.

THIS IS NOT WHAT I MEANT.

OUR USUAL SPOT, TOMORROW. 10 AM.

"Mom!" Imogen finally cut in, desperate to be alone and collect her thoughts. "Can we please talk about this after you've calmed down? Fighting won't get us anywhere."

Sylvia grunted, slamming the bedroom door on her way out. The echo of the front door banging came a moment later.

Imogen sighed and sank to the floor, drawing her knees up to her chest. Her mother rarely got enough sleep, which often led to her being short tempered and irritable. When they were younger, before life grew too expensive for anything other than survival mode, Sylvia and Imogen were close. They used to go see the Hollywood sites like Grauman's Theater or the Walk of Fame together. Now, inflation made the cost of everything go up. Their money didn't stretch nearly as far as they needed it to, and the workload drove Sylvia to exhaustion.

She couldn't let it get to her. Imogen would make a better apology in the morning by cooking Sylvia a real breakfast and letting her sleep in the bedroom rather than the couch. Fresh sheets on a real pillow could do wonders for her mother's mood.

For now, Imogen focused on cleaning herself up and then helping Austin get ready for bed. Even though she knew it meant the tv would run all night long, she let him settle into his twin bed with his favorite kids' movie, ensuring he would stay contentedly in his room. His eyes were already starting to droop by the time she flicked the light switch and closed the door behind her.

Once she determined the front door was securely locked and all the lights were off, Imogen crept back into her bedroom and knelt to take her Dolian Crawford scrapbook out from under the bed. After nearly a decade's worth of articles on his career, it was really more of an enormous binder than anything else. Imogen made it her personal mission to collect every news article on Dolian she could find. Everything was meticulously stored with plastic sheet covers and dividers identifying the month and year of publication. It was the biggest reason Sylvia always accused Imogen of stalking.

"It's not normal to keep things like this!" she always said.

With the flip of each page, his smoldering looks, powerful eyes, and tight cheekbones set Imogen's mind at ease. This was the man who haunted her dreams. There was always a Dolian Crawford movie to make her feel better, to make her feel seen in a world that desperately wanted to forget her. Nobody cared when the silent nurse-maids, the rejects, the lowlifes remained invisible. Outside of Austin, Imogen doubted anyone would notice if she were gone, not even her mother. Yet, looking at Dolian's photographs from the pages of magazines and newspapers made her feel a recognition deep in her soul. *Here is someone who cares!* her spirit cried after the turn of every page. *He sees YOU!*

Catharsis settled over her, making Imogen's body finally relax. Once she was done with the Contact tomorrow, she would go to the library to print out more articles to add to her collection. And for the first time ever Imogen could see one of her own articles added to her Dolian collection. That thought alone was enough to make her sigh in contentment.

All the tension returned to her neck and shoulders as Imogen read through one of the familiar articles. It was a piece done in *Teen Vogue* in the earlier days of his career, where Dolian actually provided a quote or two to include in the interview. This quote in particular always conjured up an image of Dolian as the quintessential husband and father; the kind of man who would provide for his wife and 2.5 offspring in a suburban house complete with white picket fence.

Reading the quote now, however, made goosebumps break out along her forearms. *"My brother, Gabriel, and I were thick as thieves growing up. He was practically my shadow, always by my side. That's how families should be for one another."*

Except at dinner Dolian made it very clear that he had no family. He didn't word it as if someone died or moved away, he distinctly told Imogen loneliness didn't bother him because he had been alone all his life. Those were very different connotations.

Imogen didn't know what to make of it. Was the quote in the article a lie? Or did he mean something else at Padre's?

She whipped out her phone, first typing a simple confirmation to the Contact so that he didn't blow up her phone with additional texts. Then she sent a request for Dolian's direct number to what she assumed to be Huxley's phone.

When the phone began to ring with an incoming FaceTime video, Imogen scrambled to sit up in bed and fluff up her hair.

It was Dolian, and he looked to be on a private plane, complete with leather seats and shiny wood paneling along the wall behind him. Small bags started to form under his eyes from the apparent lack of sleep, but he gave Imogen a bright smile as he greeted her.

"This was simply easier," he explained. "You can always reach me through this number as well since Huxley's always nearby. What's wrong?"

Imogen chewed on her bottom lip, suddenly too shy to ask the question outright. What if his brother died in a horrible accident that was too difficult for Dolian to talk about? What if she made him relive trauma because of her pestering questions?

The nagging feeling in her gut wouldn't abate, however. "Do you have a brother?" she finally asked.

Dolian chuckled lightly. "If you're asking me to set up one of your girlfriends with someone, I hate to tell you, but I'm one of a kind."

She shook her head. "No, I'm serious. Do you have a brother? Named Gabriel?"

"I'm an only child, Imogen. Why do you ask?"

Nagging progressed to downright clawing as her stomach twisted into knots. There was no way to frame her next question without it making her sound like a lunatic. "Then why did you say you have a brother named Gabriel?"

"I never said such a thing!" Dolian looked perplexed, his brow wrinkled in confusion. "Where is this coming from?"

"An article in a September issue of *Teen Vogue* from 2017," explained Imogen. "You talk about your brother and how close you were as kids."

To her surprise, Dolian laughed again. "If that's your source, we've found the problem! Those rag mags never get things right! Their journalists are phony, at best. They probably just made up a quote to help sell the issue."

While his answer made sense, Imogen found it hard to believe that a magazine loosely associated with Anna Wintour herself would so drastically compromise journalistic integrity by committing libel. "Okay," Imogen weakly replied. "I guess that makes sense."

"Darling, I promise, the last thing I would ever want to do is lie to you," Dolian assured her, making her blush. "But I'm on my way to attend the final premiere for *Agent Reckless* in Hong Kong before heading down to Australia for two weeks to tackle some last minute reshoots on my next project. I'll let you know the moment I return to L.A."

"Oh. Okay." She didn't realize they were on close enough terms that she could know his schedule. He spoke to her almost as if they were dating...not that Imogen had any frame of reference for that. None of her high school crushes compared to Dolian Crawford, so none of them ever got more than a passing wave in the hall from her.

"Get some sleep," Dolian advised her gently. "You've had a rough day."

"So have you!" countered Imogen.

He gave her a tight smile. "Yes, but I'm Dolian Crawford. Rough days are all I know."

ELEVEN

"Dolian Crawford has the skin of a chameleon, allowing him to transfigure into whatever role he chooses. Drama, comedy, avant-garde—it matters not, for he can do it all."
-Bryan Denison, Hollywood historian

Fluffy blueberry pancakes, made from scratch, have the uncanny ability to warm anyone's heart. A heaping stack of them, still hot from the griddle, topped with butter and a cascade of blueberry syrup mollified Sylvia the next morning in a way that no words ever could. While she ate, Imogen filled her mother in on the events that led to her photograph all over the internet. She conveniently left out the Contact and the two murders tied to the *Agent Reckless* movie premiere.

In the end, Sylvia looked even more worried than before. "I don't like the sounds of this, Imogen," she began. "How did he get your address to send you a phone? Why are you getting such special privileges when all these other women throw themselves at him?"

Imogen frowned at the imagery, but cleared the breakfast plates to hide the expression from her mother. "I'm sure the security team had my address on file somehow."

Except, she couldn't remember ever filling out a form with a mailing address on it.

Sylvia sighed, giving up the fight. "You're an adult now, so I can't stop you. But I strongly disagree with everything about this situation! You know I've always thought Dolian was as fake as a three dollar bill."

That was true. From the moment Imogen melted over her first Dolian Crawford film, her mother sat beside her, shaking her head and swearing there was something wrong with him. She could never articulate why, but made no effort to hide her disdain for Imogen's obsession.

"Well, it sounds like he's out of the country for a little while, so I've just gotta lay low," Imogen replied brightly.

Sylvia rolled her eyes. "If I could make you do that, we wouldn't be in this mess! I'm going to bed. I have to be at the diner for the lunch shift in a few hours." Wearily, she rose from the miniature kitchen table and shuffled back to the bedroom where Imogen had already vacuumed the bed and put on clean linens.

Imogen glanced at the clock on the microwave before rushing to find Austin's shoes. They needed to leave for the bus stop right away if she was going to make it to the Contact in time.

After Austin settled in at the Day Center, Imogen caught another bus to The Majestic. The fiasco yesterday taught her to dress incognito if she had to be around anyone associated with entertainment, so today she wore a loose fitting green maxi dress and a straw hat with a wide brim. The hat was big enough that she could tuck her hair inside, further concealing her appearance. More oversized sunglasses completed the look to obscure her face.

She kept her eyes on her sandals as she made her way through the lobby and into the bar, refusing to look anyone in the face if it risked recognition. Still, paranoia crept up her spine, an unsettling feeling that she was being watched. Every whisper had to do with Dolian Crawford and the gold-digging celebrity gossip blogger, and no amount of wardrobe changes could hide her from public scrutiny.

The moment she stepped up to the payphone at The Majestic, a piercing cry rang out as the phone rocked in its cradle. Imogen hardly dared to breathe as she answered, "Yes?"

"You've gone and made a mess of things, haven't you?" The Contact's voice was as gruff and patronizing as ever.

"Good morning to you, too," Imogen muttered.

"The time for pleasantries is long gone," he replied. "You've made a name for yourself in a bad way, Glenda."

"I had no way of knowing he would be in that coffee shop!" Imogen hated the way he scolded her like a child.

The Contact sighed. "You shouldn't have been there to begin with. I told you to issue a retraction, not continue to chase gossipmongers in Beverly Hills."

A temper like she never felt before flared in Imogen's heart. He had never belittled her blog like that before, and the insinuation that she needed to follow his orders for her articles rather than choosing her own topics needled her.

"For your information, I've already gotten email offers

from dozens of potential sponsors! That article did exactly what I wanted it to—it put me on the map!" she spit back.

"Yeah, and how long until the cops find you on the map to talk to you about Evette Coleman's murder, huh? Especially now that everyone's speculating you're actually *dating* Dolian Crawford?" His accusations sent an involuntary shudder down her spine. She had momentarily forgotten about Evette Coleman, and the security guard, for that matter.

The Contact interpreted her silence as understanding. "Glenda, you're a nobody at the bottom of the food chain in a complex, incestuous system. The underbelly of Hollywood is dark, ugly, and depressing. The sooner they find a way to pin a murder on you rather than tarnish some golden boy's reputation, the sooner they can go back to their meaningless, excessive lives. You, Glenda my dear, are expendable."

His words played over and over in her mind on the bus ride home. Austin noticed how mentally checked out Imogen was and started clapping his hands in front of her face repeatedly, annoying the other passengers, but she couldn't get her brain to focus on anything other than the Contact's warning.

Was there more to the story of Evette's murder? Imogen didn't want to poke around and draw attention to herself, but she also didn't want to run the risk of being implicated. So many people saw their unpleasant exchange in the lobby of the theater. And like the Contact pointed out, far more people would be willing to protect Dolian's reputation than Imogen's.

There was also the matter of Jesse Ramirez's murder, the security guard who broke her phone. While it was an accident, those tended to get exaggerated in Hollywood. And Imogen had no idea who else might have seen their exchange and reported it. All eyes were on Dolian that night, so when he swooped in to save her, there was a very good chance that others noticed.

The flights of stairs to their apartment had never defeated her more. Step after weary step had Imogen overanalyzing every detail of that night, volleying back and forth between investigating the murders herself and simply letting sleeping dogs lie.

A choice she no longer had to make, she realized, when Austin gleefully shouted at the top of the stairs. Two police officers flanked a man in crisp jeans and an open button down, the shiny badge on his hip matching that of the officers.

"Imogen Reilly?" the man asked. "I'm Detective Arash Davani. I have a few questions for you."

TWELVE

"I would do anything for Dolian Crawford! If he needs a kidney, a liver, or even my heart—it's his!
-@D0lianCLuv6969

A mouth drier than the Mojave Desert was not the ideal way to gulp down nerves, which Imogen discovered as she stared into the chocolate brown eyes of Detective Davani. He waited patiently next to her front door, hands casually placed on his hips, as he took in her appearance. There was nothing in his expression to indicate the conclusion of his appraisal, yet Imogen felt lacking just the same.

Austin continued to clap and wave at the officers. One of them, a woman who didn't look much older than Imogen, smiled and waved back, causing Austin to whoop with delight.

A tiny sliver of relief set in when all three police officers laughed at his excitement.

"I wish we always got this kind of welcome," the female officer muttered to her partner. He chuckled appreciatively in response.

"Are you Imogen Reilly?" the detective prompted her again.

She jumped. Now was not the time to let her mind wander.

"Yes, Detective, I'm Imogen. Please, come inside."

It took over a minute to unlock all the locks on the door and when Austin realized the officers were coming inside with them, he bounced on the balls of his feet and refused to leave the doorway. He kept repeating the "ka" sound, which Imogen explained was Austin's way of saying the word, "cop." After she managed to get her brother in far enough to shut the door, the uniformed officers quickly walked around the perimeter of the living room/kitchen combo.

"There's nobody else here," Imogen offered quietly. She'd seen enough police raids for drugs and guns at neighbors' houses growing up to know what they were doing. Her Compton address alone was enough to instill distrust with the police. "Nobody in our home uses, nobody sells, and we can't have any weapons because of Austin. Would anyone like some water?"

To her surprise, Detective Davani snickered. "I can see you're familiar with police protocol."

She shrugged.

"How about we have my partners here sit over there with the big guy, and you and I can have a seat here in the kitchen so we can chat." While the wording may have suggested an invitation, there was no question attached.

Satisfied that the officers were being kind to Austin as he animatedly showed them his drawings, Imogen sat down, facing the living room. Detective Davani pulled the chair out next to the linoleum bistro table so that he sat perpendicular to Imogen, giving him the ability to see into the living room and the front door.

"So," he began, "I'm assuming Austin is a relative?"

Imogen crossed her arms over her chest. "He's my little brother. How can I help you, sir?"

If the detective thought her rude, he didn't show it. A charming smile displaying white teeth against rich, brown skin appeared. "Do you have any idea why a detective with the LAPD might want to talk to you?"

Her hesitation no doubt spoke volumes. Imogen wasn't sure if she would be implicated more by remaining silent or acknowledging the Evette Coleman case. She settled on another noncommittal shrug.

"What can you tell me about Evette Coleman?" Davani inquired.

"She was the lead anchor on *Movie News Now*," Imogen quietly replied. Making eye contact with the detective only made her heartbeat faster, so she focused on a chip on the edge of the tabletop.

"Oh, come on," Davani urged. "You clearly know more than that."

"I beg your pardon?"

"*Was*," he repeated. "You said Evette Coleman *was* the lead anchor."

Imogen's cheeks flushed with embarrassment. "Her death has been all over the news."

The detective leaned forward to rest his forearms on the table. "Have you been reading gossip blogs or news articles?"

Her anger flared at his insult. Everyone always had to put down people like her, as if there was something demeaning about her profession. But if you placed the setting in Regency England and wrote a book series about it, Netflix would take it straight to the bank. Defending herself grew tiresome and she was in no mood to do so now.

"Detective, are we going to talk in riddles all day or can you actually get to the point?" Imogen growled through clenched teeth.

He grinned, clearly enjoying that he got under her skin. "Where were you this past Wednesday evening?"

She sighed. "At the *Agent Reckless* movie premiere. As a member of the press," she added pointedly.

Detective Davani pulled a small, leatherbound notebook from his jeans pocket. A pencil nub rested between the pages, which he used to jot down a note. "Anything exciting happen?"

"Did anything exciting happen at the world premiere of this summer's blockbuster?" Imogen repeated incredulously. "Do you even hear yourself?"

He laughed, holding up his hands in defeat. "Okay, probably not the best thing to ask. Did you come into contact with Evette Coleman at the premiere?"

The ghost of the detective's laugh might have been etched on his face, but there was no warmth in his eyes. They were shrewdly calculating her every move. Imogen sat up straighter and glared at him.

"Yes, I came into contact with her at the premiere. We had two brief conversations, one of which went south. There were plenty of witnesses who would have told you this information."

Nodding, Detective Davani scribbled something else in his notebook. "And what else would they have told me?"

"That I ran out before the movie even started because of my shame," Imogen admitted. Hearing the words out loud made her relive the humiliation all over again. She shoved her hands under her thighs to dry.

His expression instantly softened and he glanced back towards Austin before asking, "Do you take care of him full time?"

Imogen swallowed thickly, hating that tears formed in the corners of her eyes. She blinked them away before nodding. "That's why I write my blog," she explained. "It allows me to do something I love and have time for Austin's needs."

The detective nodded in understanding. "What happened after you left the premiere?"

"I raced back here because our mom had to go to work. She works overnight at a nursing home in Long Beach." She sucked in a shaky breath before adding, "I was here with Austin all night. He can't be left alone, given his condition."

Davani made a few more notes in his journal. "Can you tell me more about the bad interaction you had with Miss Coleman?"

Her sigh was heavy as her shoulders sank. She wanted to be honest, but not incriminating. "Evette wasn't particularly impressed with me and she made her feelings known. It's hard to break into this business. People tend to look down on you," Imogen added pointedly again.

Detective Davani gave her a sheepish grin. "Fair enough. Did you see her there with anyone?"

"No, but I wasn't paying much attention to her. I was a bit...emotional." Imogen watched enough crime shows with Austin to know that any kind of feelings could be twisted around to insinuate a motive, and while this wasn't a silly good cop/bad cop routine, she was afraid of saying the wrong thing. Yes, she ran away upset. No, that didn't make her a killer.

The detective merely nodded again and scribbled a few more notes down. "Is there anything you'd like to tell me?"

Imogen wanted to ask about the security guard, but didn't want to draw attention to the fact that she knew about another murder related to the premiere. As she chewed her bottom lip, debating the point like a tennis match inside her head, her cell phone buzzed loudly in her purse.

"Excuse me," Imogen mumbled, pulling out her phone to silence it only to inhale sharply when she saw Huxley's phone number coming in for a video call. Dolian had to be on the line! Since his filming schedule was so chaotic, there was a very good chance ignoring this call would mean Imogen lost the ability to talk to him today.

"I'm so sorry, Detective, but I need to take this for just a moment," Imogen pleaded.

Davani waved her toward the hallway. "Of course. Do you mind if I take a look around?"

Imogen minded very much, but with the pressure of answering Dolian's call and her uncertainty of what was permissible, she didn't have a way to say no. "Um, sure. It will just be a second!"

She clicked the green button the moment she stood up from the bistro table, rounding the corner to the hallway in the next step. Dolian's chiseled face filled the screen, his blue eyes electric. It might have been a wig for filming or simply a new haircut, but his dark brown locks were cropped shorter, though a bit tousled, like he just ran his fingers through them. The room around him appeared dark, and Imogen melted at the prospect of him beginning or ending his day by talking to her.

"Hi!" she whispered breathlessly.

Dolian scowled. "Who is that behind you?"

Imogen peered over her right shoulder, where the detective stood near the front door watching her. "Just somebody here to see me," she offered weakly. Telling Dolian about the investigation didn't feel like the right thing to say. She wasn't even sure what kind of relationship they had, and she didn't want to start running to him with every detail of her life. "Can I call you back in a few minutes?"

Dolian's brows furrowed. The shadows cast across his face almost made him look villainous. "I can't talk in a few minutes. Enjoy your night." With the slash of his arm, the call ended.

Detective Davani stepped forward. "Was that Dolian Crawford on the phone?"

The entire situation rattled Imogen, and she wrapped her arms around her waist to fortify herself against the tears that threatened. Rather than answer the detective, Imogen inquired, "Are we done here? I need to help Austin get cleaned up."

If he sensed the sudden tension in the room, Davani didn't show it. He whipped a business card out of his shirt pocket, handing it to her between two fingers. "Keep in touch if you think of anything else," Davani instructed.

The two other officers flanked the door as they all left.

Austin pouted, disappointed to lose his new friends. Davani angled his head back inside and said, "Oh, and Ms. Reilly? I'll be in touch again soon," before closing the door firmly behind him.

Nights like tonight made Imogen sad that she couldn't drink.

THIRTEEN

"A good mystery is always exciting, but a mystery that looks like Dolian Crawford? That'll get your blood flowing!"
-Todd Crandell, US Weekly

Sleep evaded Imogen worse than ever before. She tossed and turned most of the night, her creative mind sending her horror story after horror story. By the time dawn seeped over the horizon, Imogen had convinced herself that she was going to the electric chair for both murders, thereby forcing her mother to be homeless because Sylvia lost all her jobs from shame while poor Austin wound up in an abusive group home that let him starve. It was the most extreme outcome imaginable considering she didn't have anything to do with either murder, but all rationality disappeared once exhaustion set in.

I need your help

Too despondent to wait for a reply from the Contact, she got up and began pacing the bedroom. *What I really need*, she thought, *is to find out more about the security guard's murder on my own.*

Was she worrying over nothing? Detective Davani was likely interviewing everyone from the premiere. After all, Evette Coleman's death was a high profile murder. Her death sent ripples of shock through the Valley. It was only natural that he covered all bases by interviewing every member of the press who was there that night.

But Imogen wasn't just there, she had a public scene with Evette. And Jesse, the security guard. Not all of the guests were as implicated. What if the Contact was right and the prosecutors chose to make her a scapegoat? There was obviously no way she could leave Austin home alone at night, but would that be an alibi for someone who didn't understand his special needs? Abled bodied people did not have much empathy for those with disabilities. They had even less for their caretakers.

It was enough to make Imogen's head spin. Getting answers was the only way to calm her growing anxiety, however. If the Contact didn't text her back in thirty minutes, she had to go seek them for herself.

Just lay low

came his reply a moment later.

Imogen shook her head, throwing her phone down on the bed in agitation. Laying low simply wasn't an option. She recalled how shrewdly Davani assessed her the day before, the haste with which he scribbled notes on her replies. No, she was much better off investigating on her own, Imogen decided.

———

Sylvia was in a good mood that morning after having a great shift at the diner the night before. She sang along off-key to Spotify as she made scrambled eggs, which made Austin laugh and dance. Imogen entered the kitchen to the joyous sounds of their revelry with surprise. It was highly unusual for Sylvia to engage with Austin like that.

"Good morning, Sunshine!" Sylvia greeted her with a smile. "Do you want anything to eat?"

Imogen shook her head. "Shouldn't you be at work?"

"The store has to have some plumbing work done, so Maury decided it wasn't worth the hassle to open today." Maury was also their landlord, who let Sylvia work at the convenience store on the bottom floor of the building in exchange for a discount on their rent. He was a terrible Scrooge, nickeling and diming every customer, vendor, and tenant to death. Imogen knew without asking that there had to be a serious issue with the plumbing for him to hire a professional in the first place.

"So what are your plans for the day?" Imogen asked. She twirled on the spot, chuckling along with her mother at how the simple act lit up Austin's face.

Sylvia slid a plate of scrambled eggs on the table. "Well, I thought I would hang out here with Austin and give you a bit of a break," she said. "I feel really bad about how we've been fighting lately."

Her mom had never done anything so considerate before.

Imogen wanted to be suspicious, but also didn't want to look a gift horse in the mouth. "Really?" she hedged. "Austin has a bit of a routine on Saturdays…"

Sylvia waved off Imogen's concerns. "I'm his mother, Imogen. I can spend the day with my son if I want to!"

An entire day to herself meant Imogen could poke around a bit and see what she discovered about the security guard's murder. She didn't want to act relieved at the day of freedom or else her mother would start to pressure her about sending Austin to a group home again. The timing of it all was a bit serendipitous.

"There are a few places I'd love to go see around town," Imogen admitted. "It would be easier if I could go see them without taking Austin."

"You should go. One of the nurses at work gave me a bag of DVD's she was getting rid of, so Austin and I are gonna have a movie marathon." Sylvia held up her hand and Austin gave her a loud high five. "As long as you're back by four so I can make it in for the dinner shift."

Imogen smiled, still hardly believing the turn of events. "I can do that. Thanks, Mom."

She waited until Austin and Sylvia were settled on the couch before slipping quietly out the front door. If he realized she was missing, Austin could go nuclear and derail her plans.

The first person Imogen needed to see was an acquaintance from high school. Labeling him as a friend would be a stretch, but Dylan Toledano had used that term when introducing her to his mom all those years ago. Dylan was a computer geek and hacking extraordinaire. He liked to brag about how the FBI and CIA kept tabs on his accounts, though Imogen never knew if it was true or not. Dylan's time in front of a computer made for poor social skills, and he could be difficult to talk to. For that reason, Imogen tended to avoid him whenever possible. But if he could hack into the LAPD files and get her some notes on both murders, she would at least have a better idea of where to begin.

Judging by the smell wafting through the gap in the door when Dylan opened it, quite some time had passed since he had last been outside. The air had a staleness to it, a lingering hint of body odor, dampness, and greasy food. He gave Imogen just enough room to slip inside the messy living area of his studio apartment before slamming the door shut behind her.

"You shouldn't be here!" Dylan hissed at her.

"Why?" she asked, surprised at his outburst.

Dylan scoffed, pointing to his wall of computer monitors. Three of them had up articles with the paparazzi photos from the coffee house. "Because you're all over the internet! I don't want to be associated with you when the Feds come knocking!" He dropped into a computer chair and whirled around to face the monitors dramatically.

The small space felt even more minuscule with all of the clutter littering the space. A futon, folded up into a couch, with a stained mattress and tattered blanket sat against the wall next to the door. Everything else in the room looked to be a mix of garbage, laundry, and old computer pieces. Hardware drives, keyboards, and sound systems all towered in various mountains that Imogen had to weave through in order to reach Dylan's monstrous computer set up. His desk sagged under the weight of Mountain Dew bottles and half-eaten takeout containers, making Imogen crinkle her nose at the foul smell of food spoiling.

She sighed. "That's why I'm here, Dyl. I need your help. Wait—could you take any of it down?"

His responding sound was a cross between a laugh and a snarl. "Of course I can take it down! That kinda thing is for amateurs!"

She scooted next to him, trying not to tip over any of the stacks of hard drives, keyboards, and fast food containers that randomly dotted the space. One of the monitors displayed a computer game, which seemed to have most of Dylan's focus at the moment as he aggressively slammed his thumb on the keys to make the character attack. A large pair of headphones with a microphone hung from his neck, signaling he was at least willing to talk to her. Dylan would slam the headset on angrily any time he wanted to end a conversation, and had done so to her many times over the years.

"So what do you really want?" Dylan asked her. Satisfied with his game, he rolled the chair further to the right and typed rapidly, his eyes glued to a string of intimidating code. Imogen never learned much in her computer classes at school. Dylan's entire setup felt like a smelly version of Penelope Garcia's.

"I need you to hack into the LAPD for me," Imogen explained. It was better to be blunt and direct with Dylan. "I need some files."

Dylan didn't even look up. "Right on!"

Imogen smiled weakly, not that Dylan noticed. "They're files from a murder investigation. For Evette Coleman and Jesse Ramirez."

"Wicked," he replied instantly.

"And I'm afraid they think I'm involved," she finished.

His hands slithered to his lap as he turned the chair to face her. "You?" Dylan inquired incredulously.

"Well...yeah." Embarrassment flamed her cheeks.

To her surprise, Dylan tilted his head back and roared with laughter. "There's no way they think that!" Continuing to chuckle, he twirled the chair back towards the monitors and resumed the game.

"Dylan," cried Imogen, "I am telling you, the detective came to my house last night!"

He rolled his eyes as he pushed away from the desk to shuffle around her towards the kitchenette. In a studio this small, all he really had was a refrigerator, sink, and a countertop just big enough for a microwave, although that was all Dylan truly needed anyway. Yanking open the fridge, Dylan pulled a two liter of Pepsi out and guzzled it straight from the bottle.

"You look like that little pixie thing from *Peter Pan*," Dylan assured her. "There's no way anyone is pegging a murder on you! Don't get your panties in a wad." He belched loudly and returned to his computer chair, once again adding to the code.

Imogen folded her arms over her chest. "Whether that's true or not, I saw both of the victims on the night of the murder. I have to know what I'm dealing with."

Dylan snorted. "Might wanna spend less time with Dolian 'Dirtbag' Crawford, then."

In all her years of obsessing over the superstar, she had never once heard him referred to as such. "Excuse me?"

"Yeah, your fancy boyfriend has the kind of money and

connections to have a lot of stuff pulled from the internet, but the dark web doesn't lie. Dolian Crawford has been accused of some nasty shit from people. Word on the street is he's got a bad temper. Beat a gardener so bad he needed reconstructive surgery. It's all hush, hush," Dylan added.

Could that possibly be true? All the years of tracking down every article, every photograph, literally anything with Dolian's name hadn't once revealed the truth about him?

Yet, how could any of that be real when she had seen firsthand how kindly he treated Austin? How he made every effort to treat her respectfully? None of it made any sense.

A large printer on a stand underneath the solitary window started spitting out paper. The sound made Imogen jump.

"That's all for you," explained Dylan without breaking eye contact with a monitor. "Everything's there. The case files, photographs of the crime scenes, all of it. Printed out a few of the eyewitness reports on Dolian Crawford, too. You might wanna watch your six with that dude."

A plastic bag filled with garbage fell over as Imogen tried to navigate her way to the printer. She could never live with all the clutter Dylan had lying around. Although he didn't offer it, when Imogen spotted a manila folder tucked under a box of spare ink cartridges, she quietly tugged it free and placed all the paperwork inside.

"Uh, thanks a ton, Dylan," she said. "I owe you one."

"Yeah, you do," he agreed with a dark chuckle, still facing the wall of computer screens. With a plop, his headset went over his ears as a sign of his dismissal. Imogen slipped back outside and expelled the breath she held. Fresh air felt marvelous after the decay of his studio.

FOURTEEN

"Dolian Crawford is not the white knight the media wants to portray him as. He is cold and cruel. I'll never work with him again."
-Zarah Mirez, assistant production coordinator

As much as she itched to sit down and read through the file right away, Dylan didn't live in the best neighborhood either. Most parts of Compton still struggled with gang violence and crime. It was one of the biggest reasons Imogen wanted to get Austin out of the area.

She hopped on the closest bus to head over to Ladera Park. They had plenty of picnic tables to sit on without running the risk of someone looking over her shoulder. Privacy was key since it was highly illegal for her to have copies of notes from an active murder investigation. The last thing she needed was for social services to rain down on their family because she got caught up in something criminal. Austin would be taken from them before she could say his name.

The case files for Evette Coleman were extensive. Detective Davani had systemically interviewed dozens of paparazzi, event coordinators, and members of the press who all attended the premiere. Several accounts reported the spat between Imogen and Evette far more dramatically than she recalled, but it was clear that everyone in attendance at *Agent Reckless* witnessed their exchange and reported it to the officers. No one reported Imogen as the victim, however. Bystanders simply alluded to an escalating verbal altercation between the two. It infuriated her that people could have such a collectively skewed recollection, but then again, that was always the case in Hollywood.

Davani's notes from his interview with Imogen weren't nearly as detailed. He repeatedly addressed her supposed attempts to "act innocent."

That's because I am! Imogen thought savagely.

They went on to add that Davani intended to follow up on her alibi, making her heart race. If they contacted her mother, Sylvia would have Austin in a group home and Imogen out on the street in record-breaking time. She desperately wished she knew what Davani meant.

Case notes on Jesse Ramirez proved what a drastic difference there was between social classes. While Evette had several dozen interviews and hundreds of crime scene photographs, Jesse's file only had two interviews. One was with his work supervisor, confirming Jesse was sent home early from the movie premiere because of "subpar performance." Imogen knew they meant incurring Dolian's wrath. It had to reflect poorly on the company to have an A-list celebrity angry with one of your employees. Nothing expounded on what the performance issue was, though, and nothing indicated Jesse had a run in with Imogen earlier in the evening.

The second interview was from the roommate who found the body in the alleyway behind their apartment building. Apparently both roommates used the back service door to the building in an effort to avoid the landlord because of their past due rent. Jesse's roommate said they both worked multiple jobs to try because they wanted to create a music app, so they rarely saw each other due to their conflicting schedule. He had no idea if Jesse knew anyone with a motive for murder.

The roommate's alibi checked out since he was at work all evening, and the detective's notes indicated they had no further leads. Imogen would be willing to bet they weren't trying very hard to find any. Eyeing the Koreatown address, she seriously doubted the police had a reason to investigate any further. People could disappear off the map in that part of L.A. and no one would bat an eye.

Glancing at her watch, Imogen determined she had enough time still to go to Jesse's building and poke around. Koreatown didn't scare her and it was still early enough in the day that not as many people would be out.

But first—she was dying to know more about Dylan's allegations against Dolian. If anyone thought he was a hair short of perfection, Imogen would set them straight or die trying. He couldn't possibly be the monster Dylan claimed him to be.

Even if she started to doubt that herself.

Judging from the notes, Davani tried-unsuccessfully-to schedule a meeting with Dolian and one of his representatives and was directed to speak to an attorney instead. That amazed Imogen since Dolian seemed so unfazed by the whole thing. He acted as though none of it mattered to him, so why wouldn't he just meet with the police to say so?

As she dug into the reports of Dolian himself, Imogen's stomach bottomed out. There were more than fifty accounts of Dolian behaving in an abusive, offensive manner. Some were simple accounts from waitstaff who served him at restaurants and found him to be rude and demanding, while others went into far more detail. Many of the low-end movie employees had poor opinions of him, reporting verbal threats, violent outbursts, and escalating altercations that often involved the employee leaving in tears. One stated she was on anxiety medication for the panic attacks he induced.

None of this can possibly be right, Imogen thought. *He was a total gentleman when I was with him!*

Except...was he? Imogen remembered how silently the waitress at the Mexican restaurant remained, how quickly she scampered around to provide Dolian's every wish. Was that borne out of fear? It felt like all the fantasies she'd nurtured about Dolian over the years evaporated before her eyes. Maybe she didn't know him as well as she thought she did.

Maybe she didn't know him at all.

FIFTEEN

"Dolian Crawford can play the villain, the good guy, and the goofy best friend all in the same movie—he's THAT good!"
-Tiktok Influencer, @MovEgal2005

Imogen stepped off the bus in Jesse Ramirez's neighborhood and cast a furtive look up and down the street. She couldn't shake the feeling that someone was watching her. No one actually seemed to pay her much attention that she could tell, but she donned her oversized sunglasses just the same. It was more of an eerie feeling that made her continually glance over her shoulder. Paranoia from the tabloids was getting to her, Imogen reasoned.

Jesse's apartment building looked like the rest of the complexes on the block, with a cheesy stereotype of Asian décor on the façade. Street vendors catcalled people walking by while older Korean grandparents sat on street stoops to watch. There were mouthwatering scents filtering out through doorways, but Imogen didn't waste the time to stop.

She snatched a quick peek over her shoulder again before slipping down the alleyway behind Jesse's building. The Ramirez case had a different detective than Evette Coleman so she didn't know who to watch out for if she were to encounter anybody. Nothing in the alley indicated any kind of crime scene investigation either. Imogen expected caution tape or a chalk outline of a body. Maybe even some dried blood splatter.

Other than an overflowing dumpster, the area looked normal. An emergency exit was propped open, likely from tenants like Jesse, but she hesitated before entering the building. It was one thing to poke around and physically look for clues. It was another entirely to interview Jesse's roommate and neighbors. While the occupants of Koreatown probably didn't know (or care) that Imogen had recently been under a microscope, there was always the risk that they did. She wasn't certain of the fallout if someone recognized her and reported her snooping.

Imogen stood there, chewing at her bottom lip while she mulled over her options, when the sound of an aluminum can skidding across the concrete made her jump. Detective Davani stood a few feet behind her, hands seemingly casually placed in his jean pockets. There was nothing casual on his face, though. His eyes were calculating, pinning her with a look that made Imogen feel guilty despite doing nothing wrong.

"Fancy seeing you here, Ms. Reilly," he said.

She took a step backward, creating more distance between them. "Are you following me?" Imogen asked.

"Just happened to be in the neighborhood. Saw you duck down here and wanted to make sure you're okay."

Davani shrugged as if it was a perfectly normal thing to do.

She scoffed. "You just *happened* to be in the neighborhood? A neighborhood where a murder recently took place?"

Davani's face piqued with interest. "Murders occur frequently in Los Angeles. I'd know that better than anyone." He gave a half-hearted chuckle. "What do you know about a murder in the area?"

Panicking at being caught in a web of her own making, Imogen took another shaky step backwards. The alleyway ended in the brick wall of the building one street over, so there was nowhere for her to turn. She wasn't prepared to answer any of the detective's questions.

"It was a hunch," suggested Imogen. A shrug indicated her indifference. "You are a homicide detective after all. Death follows you everywhere."

Davani cocked his head to the side as he contemplated her answer. He had just opened his mouth to reply when a gravelly voice interrupted.

"There you are! I've been looking everywhere for you, Imogen!" Dolian stalked down the alley, holding up his arms in relief. He brushed past the detective briskly, nearly knocking him over, in his haste to get to Imogen. Embracing her like she was a lost puppy, Dolian's arms around her felt like steel pythons as he lavished her with attention. His eyes turned stormy as he perused Davani from head to toe. "Who are you?"

With eyes as wide as half dollars, Detective Davani blinked at the movie star, totally dumbstruck. "You're Dolian Crawford," he said incredulously. "In a dirty alleyway. In Koreatown."

Imogen idly wondered if she was going to have her first experience fainting. "What are you doing here?" she hissed in a whisper to Dolian.

The smile he gave her didn't reach his eyes. "I came for you, of course."

While Imogen wanted to feel butterflies erupt from his statement, all she could think about were the reports of Dolian's character Dylan found on the dark web. His words didn't sound romantic as much as they sent a shiver down her spine.

"How did you know to find me here?" she panted. They barely knew each other, and this was so far outside of her usual haunts, that the entire thing made no sense. Warning bells rang in her head that she needed to be on high alert.

As if sensing her rising panic, Dolian squeezed her waist. "I'll explain in a moment," he whispered. "Ah, sir, if you don't mind, I'll be taking my girlfriend home now. This was all just a big miscommunication."

"A 'miscommunication?'" Davani repeated, using finger air quotes. "You and I have very different definitions of what that means."

Dolian's returning smile dripped with condescension. "Yes, well, I don't have time to give you a vocabulary lesson. Imogen and I will be leaving now." He laced his fingers through hers and all but yanked her forward. She brushed past the detective, mumbling an incoherent apology, as she powerwalked to keep up with Dolian's lanky stride.

Once they emerged back on the busy street and crossed onto the next block, Imogen recognized Huxley standing beside a black SUV. She finally tugged her fingers from Dolian's grasp and stopped abruptly.

"How did you know where I was, Dolian?" Imogen indignantly demanded. Never one for physical fitness, their quick escape nearly did her in, along with the adrenaline from all the fear coursing through her body. She bent over, hands on her knees, and tried to gulp lungs full of air.

Glancing around at the curious passers-by who walked and openly gawked, he leaned towards her to insist, "I won't do this on the street for the world to hear. Get in the car, Imogen!"

"No!" she shot back angrily. The warning bells were now full on sirens and she intended to listen this time.

For two whole seconds Imogen actually believed it worked. But then his expression turned thunderous. Wrapping an arm around her tight enough to pin her arms to her sides, Dolian shoved Imogen inside the back of the vehicle. Huxley snapped the door shut before she could blink.

"Get your hands off me!" Imogen screamed.

"Don't ever tell me 'no,'" Dolian warned her, his voice low and menacing. "It's my least favorite word."

She rolled her eyes and scooted farther away from him. "That's not how the world works, Dolian."

He huffed in annoyance. "You don't become an award winning actor by accepting the word 'no.'" Settling back into the smooth leather seat, Dolian pulled his sunglasses off and grabbed an iPad lying on the seat in front of him. "You're lucky I found you when I did. You have no business being over here, Imogen."

It unnerved her to hear him scold her like a child. There wasn't anything wrong with where he found her. She was trying to clear both of their names, for crying out loud! Not that Dolian seemed concerned on either front.

"Tell me how you knew where I was!" Imogen insisted.

He glared at her. "I had your phone line added to my plan so that you didn't have to worry about a bill. When you didn't respond to any of Huxley's texts, I turned on the 'Find my iPhone' feature. You had no business being in that alley!"

Imogen huffed in frustration. "And you had no business adding my phone to your plan *or* using it to track me! Don't you realize what an invasion of privacy that is? You, of all people!"

Dolian adjusted his body so that he faced her head on in the small space of the vehicle. His muscular arm spread across the top of the seats, his hand lining up perfectly with the height of her neck. A vein in his forehead throbbed, cautioning her against what was to come, but he remained preternaturally still.

"If it's privacy you seek, I can certainly accommodate that. Not a soul would know where to find you."

Imogen could barely breathe. He never seemed more dangerous to her than he did in that moment. As she tried to regulate her heartbeat, Imogen whispered, "I'm sorry, Dolian."

The apology satisfied him. Instantly, his body language relaxed and his usual, charming smile stretched across his face. "Good. We have a gala to go to this evening. We're on our way to pick up your dress."

Her mouth dropped open. "I *cannot* go with you! Are you insane?!"

His dark demeanor returned. "No," Dolian ground out. "I am not."

She shook her head, realizing she needed to choose her words with care. They were confined in a small space and no one knew where she was. If Dolian was as angry and violent as Dylan's reports said, Imogen needed to find a safe place to live, not provoke him.

"I didn't mean it like that," amended Imogen. "But I can't go to a gala. We shouldn't even be seen together right now."

Dolian snorted. "Attending an event together isn't going to make the media storm go away, Imogen. Trust me, it's better that we're seen." He picked up the tablet again and resumed scrolling as if the subject was closed.

Tears prickled at the corner of her eyes. Imogen was completely helpless. Dolian already told her he refused to accept "no" as an answer. How do you win an argument with an immovable object?

"My mom has to work tonight," she said quietly, looking at her hands as they fidgeted in her lap. "I have to stay with Austin."

Dolian glanced up at her, his gaze thoughtful. "Let me talk to her. It's important to me that you're with me tonight." Leaning forward, his eyes searched her beseechingly, a stray lock of his hair dropping down.

Her brain and her hormones were waging war. On the one hand, Imogen knew that she needed to get to the bottom of the murder investigations. She didn't want to be a suspect, even if she knew her innocence. LAPD needed to know, too. And until she dug a little deeper on the accounts of the movie star's supposedly brutish behavior, Imogen needed to keep her guard up.

But this was Dolian Crawford. As much as the reports gave her a reason to be suspicious, he was the object of all her fantasies. Teenage Imogen only survived high school because she fantasized about this moment—the chance to go on a date with a celebrity like Dolian. He looked every bit a dream at that moment, with his bright smile, tan skin, and artfully tousled hair. It was important enough to him that she go that he was willing to face Sylvia, which Imogen imagined as a modernized interpretation of David vs. Goliath. Only which one was David and which one was Goliath was anyone's guess. Imogen didn't favor the odds for either person.

"Huxley, we're going to Imogen's apartment," Dolian instructed.

"Yes, sir," Huxley replied, then leaned over to whisper to the driver.

As the partition raised between the rows, Imogen whispered, "Does your driver not speak?"

Dolian gave her a proud smile. "He just doesn't speak to me. No one does unless Huxley says so." He returned his attention to the iPad, letting his hand casually graze her arm until it rested on top of hers.

Imogen gulped, but she wasn't sure if it was from nerves or from excitement. This was a momentous occasion. She was going on a date with Dolian Crawford!

SIXTEEN

"I wish all my actors showed the level of dedication that Dolian has. The man is a machine—nothing gets in his way."
-Sterling Olivier, director

From the moment they walked in the door, Imogen knew the whole thing was a terrible idea. There was an accident on the freeway that extended their drive and they barely made it before Sylvia's four o'clock cut off. She was already wearing her diner uniform and apron when Imogen walked in, Dolian a half pace behind her.

Having a movie star as recognizable and handsome as Dolian Crawford in her cramped, rundown apartment felt a bit like stepping into the Twilight Zone. His entire persona was so overwhelming and impressive that it made their surroundings hazy and out of focus. Dolian could outshine the sun. Thankfully, he didn't comment on the small space or the shabbiness of the building in general. He was smiling and gracious as soon as they stepped inside.

Austin gleefully clapped and enveloped Dolian in a hug. Imogen's heart skipped a beat to see Dolian return the hug, greeting Austin like an old friend. It was so rare for people to engage with him the way Dolian did that the simple act immediately restored him to his pedestal in Imogen's eyes. None of those so-called "encounters" with Dolian could be true. Nobody who was that kind to a young person with Down Syndrome could be so belligerent to a production assistant that they burst into tears. And if it had happened, there must have been a good reason. Dolian was simply too perfect to do something that mean.

Sylvia, however, looked livid. As soon as she spotted the movie star, her arms folded across her chest and she pinned him with a look that reminded Imogen of a snake before it sank its fangs into their prey. There was no way she would let Imogen off the hook for tonight.

"Mrs. Reilly, I'm Dol—" he began, but Sylvia cut him off immediately.

"It's 'Miss Reilly.' Always has been, always will be," Sylvia snapped. "And I know who you are. Imogen's been obsessed with you for years."

Imogen wanted to step into a pit of dynamite. Her entire face burned with embarrassment at her mom's crass statement, but when she glanced at Dolian, he beamed at Sylvia's words. Like it was the best compliment he had ever received.

"That's delightful to hear!" he replied.

Her glare turned on Imogen. "I have to leave for work now or I'll be late. Why the hell is he here?"

Imogen frantically looked between her mother's murderous gaze and Dolian's confusion before grabbing her mother by the hand and pulling her back into their shared bedroom. "Mom, *why* are you doing this?!" she hissed in a whisper. "That is *Dolian Crawford* out there!"

Sylvia rolled her eyes. "I don't care if it's the fucking Pope, Imogen! I have to work!" Unlike her daughter, Sylvia didn't bother to keep her voice down. Imogen cringed at how loudly her statement echoed through the apartment. Their walls were paper thin.

"Mom, he wants me to go somewhere with him tonight," Imogen began, but stopped when her mother's face turned bright red with rage.

"I'M NOT LOSING MY JOB BECAUSE YOU CAN'T GROW UP!" screamed Sylvia. "WAKE UP, LITTLE GIRL! Are you out of your mind, Imogen?! This is how we put food on the table! This is how I pay for the internet you need for your silly, little blog! I'M GOING TO WORK!"

Sylvia threw open the bedroom door with enough force for the doorknob to crack into the drywall. She stormed down the hallway, Imogen hot on her heels, and stopped short at Dolian's domineering form in front of the door. His hands were tight fists on his hips, and judging by the look of fury he wore, he heard every word of their exchange in the bedroom.

"How dare you speak to your daughter like that!" Dolian's gravelly voice was glacial. He didn't yell, but he didn't need to. The threat in his tone was so evident that Imogen wanted to take a step backward. "Imogen's writing will set your family up for life."

Without so much as a blink, Sylvia turned back towards Imogen and said, "Hey, you might wanna call off your attack dog here or you're not gonna have a place to sleep tonight.

Quit being so fucking selfish, Imogen!" She pushed past Dolian enough to slip out the front door.

Imogen realized by Austin's crestfallen face that Sylvia hadn't even said goodbye to him. That broke her heart far more than Sylvia's insults or threats to Imogen.

Dolian's eyes narrowed into slits as he glared at the door. The tension was mounting so high in the confined space that Imogen half-expected the walls to crack from the pressure. Dolian had to take several deep breaths before he turned towards her with his usual smile. He offered Austin an even bigger one, improving Imogen's mood.

"Well, it looks like Austin will get to join us," Dolian announced smoothly. "Let me just step out and make a few phone calls. I'm assuming you'll need to pack a bag for him?" he asked Imogen pointedly.

She nodded quickly. The entire invitation already felt so surreal, but to have Dolian's solution be including her brother with their plans made Imogen feel like she was floating. And the last thing she would have predicted.

People rarely understood what it was like for the caretaker of someone with disabilities. They live in a constant state of high alert and bubbling anxiety. There is so much fear involved because any moment could lead to a disaster. Imogen learned that back at the babysitter's pool before she was even old enough to care for Austin. And while she loved and accepted all of her brother's quirks and needs, she had long since made peace with the fact that there would never be anyone else in her life who would. She never minded the possibility that it would be Austin and Imogen against the world until now. Now Dolian Crawford, of all people, showed her that having someone else to shoulder some of the responsibilities could be freeing. Austin didn't need to be excluded, therefore excluding her by extension, when they could both simply live like abled-bodied people.

Freedom felt sensational.

"Guess what, buddy?" she whispered conspiratorially to Austin. "We're gonna go with Dolian and do something fun tonight!"

Austin's demeanor instantly changed. A wide smile stretched across his face as he jumped in place. He turned and pointed towards his coloring books, grunting excitedly.

"Yeah, we'll bring some of your books. Can you get your backpack and choose the ones you want?"

Clapping his hands in delight, Austin pushed her out of the way in his haste to get to the backpack in his bedroom. Imogen laughed at his excitement. It was so rare to see.

Dolian stepped back inside at that moment, and the sight of Imogen's laughter seemed to make his body relax. A smooth smile fell into place as his shoulders fell. "You're not upset?"

She smiled, stepping closer to him. Her happiness made her want to kiss him, but Imogen had never been the kind of woman bold enough to make the first move. "How could I be upset? I get to have a night out with my two favorite people."

"You mean your favorite person and your brother," amended Dolian with a grin.

Imogen laughed. "Sure, that works, too!"

Heart pounding, Imogen realized Dolian's face inched towards hers. His eyes were light and full of hunger…a hunger he felt for her.

The oxygen slowly started to leak out of the room and Imogen could have sworn the ground fell away beneath her.

Dolian was going to kiss her again. He was in her living room, and he wanted to kiss her. She licked her lips, closing her eyes as she waited for him to finally reach her mouth. A tickle of his breath reached her lips…

Then Austin ran back into the room, whooping with glee. Imogen jumped away like she had been struck by a live wire. Chest heaving, she drew back a few feet, the air turning to ice as the distance between them widened. Dolian panted, gazing at Imogen with such adoration and longing that she nearly lost her balance. He couldn't possibly be looking that way at *her*.

Imogen shook her head to clear the brain fog before turning to Austin with a smile. "Are you all ready to go?" It was hard to mask the excitement in her voice. For a movie star like Dolian to be so accommodating and understanding gave her hope, and that was something Imogen hadn't felt in a long time. Wherever they were going, it was sure to become a core memory for her.

When they got downstairs, she was surprised to see a sleek stretch limousine replaced the SUV. Huxley was there and apparently acting as the driver because he opened the door for them, then rounded the car to enter the driver's seat. Austin was so delighted he bounced in his seat and cheered.

"Yay is right, buddy!" Imogen beamed at him. It was rare to ever see Austin this happy.

Dolian slid closer to her, casually wrapping his arm around her shoulders as if it were the most natural gesture in the world. He smiled at Austin's antics, too, though it was the tight smile that didn't quite reach his eyes. Imogen immediately felt guilty; after all, Dolian had planned this evening for the two of them, and Austin was a lot for a third wheel.

"I can't thank you enough," she whispered.

He leaned over to kiss the top of her head. "You'll never have to," vowed Dolian.

There was definitely no truth to those eyewitness accounts Dylan gave her. Dolian was being a perfect gentleman and treating her like a rare treasure. Imogen finally realized what it meant to be cherished, and her love for the man only grew. Dolian Crawford was special. Legendary.

And for the time being, he was all hers.

SEVENTEEN

"The man can get anything he wants because he can afford anything he wants. Dolian Crawford will be the highest paid actor of all time, mark my words."
-Adam Westbank, Wall Street Journal

To her surprise, the limo took them to The Majestic. Austin remained quiet on the drive there, but squealed in delight when they exited the vehicle to find Charles Sullivan, also known as Sully, one of Austin's favorite workers from the Day Center, standing there waiting for them. He had on a suit and tie, a much more formal outfit than Imogen had ever seen on him.

Dolian's phone rang the moment they disembarked, and he stepped away to speak to the person privately. He waved her forward, indicating she should continue inside without him.

"Sully, what are you doing here?" Imogen asked.

"When Dolian Crawford calls, you answer," Sully leaned

in and whispered conspiratorially with a grin. "Never thought my line of work would get me to such fancy places!"

Imogen had no idea what that meant. Why would Dolian need Sully for anything? She continued inside to the lobby where Huxley waited with a team of three women. Huxley merely nodded to her, not saying a word. Dolian joined them, wrapping an arm around her waist.

"Perfect timing, Huxley," Dolian greeted. "Let's go." He steered them towards the gold plated elevators, the trio following, and Sully and Austin bringing up the rear.

"Where are we going? What's happening?" Imogen inquired. Sully spoke animatedly with Austin, but she could feel the judgmental stares of the women. They pierced her back with their jealousy.

"We're going up to my suite so that we can get ready for the gala tonight. These ladies will handle your hair, makeup, and wardrobe. You have a collection of dresses to choose from," Dolian explained with a smile. He gazed down at her, watching her reaction.

Imogen was awestruck. "You have a suite at The Majestic?" she sputtered.

He chuckled. "Of course I do. I own the hotel."

She tried not to look stunned at the news. Dolian was one of the highest paid actors in Hollywood. It made sense that he invested that money into other ventures, thereby earning more revenue. But she couldn't imagine news like that not being common knowledge in the entertainment world. Or at least to her, given how she tracked his every move.

The elevator doors opened directly into the living area of what Imogen assumed was the penthouse. Large windows showcased a breathtaking view of the Valley, all encased in tiered, teal velvet curtains. Overall, the room mimicked the old Hollywood glamour of the rest of the hotel. An ornate gold mirror that was nearly floor to ceiling leaned against the wall behind the art deco styled sofa. A five tiered crystal chandelier hung from the center of the room, serving as the main focal point. The walls were all a creamy white, with black and white photographs of famous actors long since passed. The rolling clothes rack and boxes of shoes looked to be the only modern things in the room. Imogen wanted to pinch herself.

"Right, so Sully, if you'll take Austin down that hallway to one of the bedrooms, my stylist will meet you down there so we can help our special guest get his tuxedo on." Dolian pointed down the hallway to the right. One of the trio stepped forward to follow them.

"And you, my dear, can follow me to the primary bedroom." Dolian laced his fingers through hers, guiding her to the left. They passed a large kitchen, complete with a dining table big enough to seat twelve, and another bedroom until they arrived in the most regal bedroom Imogen could imagine.

The tiered velvet curtains hung in this bedroom as well, but these were in a rich emerald color. Everything was gold plated, reflecting the room back to them. The four poster bed looked like an Alaskan king, covered with more emerald velvet. A white fur rug looked plush enough that Imogen wanted to lay down on it, but the director's chair and three-sided floor length mirror were clearly meant for her. Two stands on either side of the chair held make up and hair products.

"Now, unfortunately we don't have much time or we will

be late, so I need to get ready myself," Dolian explained. He sounded genuinely apologetic. "I'm leaving you in good hands. Mariah and Lucy are the very best. Talia will be back shortly with dresses for you to choose from."

"Well, where are you going to be?" Imogen suddenly felt shy and awkward. Everything about the space and the stylists seemed so glamorous, making her stick out like a sore thumb. She was just as self-conscious now as she was at the *Agent Reckless* premiere. The entire situation was a pampered luxury to her whereas it constituted a lifestyle for Dolian. Imogen could never get used to it.

"Just here, in the bathroom," Dolian assured her, jutting a thumb over his shoulder at the door behind him. "I have my own stylist waiting for me."

Imogen nodded. "Gregory, I know."

His eyebrows peaked, a grin crossing his tan face. "And how do you know that?"

Oh, shit! Imogen thought. She racked her brain for a reasonable way to explain it, but finally settled on a partial truth. "I read a magazine where they were speculating on which stylist you favored. Gregory Polin was who the article decided on."

In reality, several news articles focused on the designers and fashion trends Dolian followed after he first made it big. Since he wouldn't talk to journalists, they had a field day with the aspects of his life for which they could glean more information. It was widely reported at the time that several of the suits Dolian wore on red carpets belonged to Gregory Polin's line. When Gregory stopped designing except for one of a kind looks only Dolian wore, it was only logical for

Imogen to make the deduction. Given Gregory's fame, Dolian had to be paying a pretty penny.

Rather than looking alarmed or disgusted—both of which would be valid feelings, Imogen surmised—Dolian looked delighted. "Have you been reading about me?"

She flushed. Her hands instantly dampened, and she wiped them on the backs of her thighs as she took a step backwards. "I have to get ready," Imogen whispered quietly, her eyes trained on her feet.

Dolian chuckled again. "Okay," he acknowledged, backing away just like her, but with a beaming smile in place.

Imogen wanted the floor to swallow her whole. Having a relationship of any kind with the actor meant she needed to keep her obsession in check. While her mother might tolerate the quirk, nobody else would find her rolodex of Dolian Crawford factoids amusing.

Thankfully, Mariah and Lucy saved her from dwelling further on her faux pas.

"So, what are we thinking for the hair?" the taller one asked.

"What color palette do you like?" the heavier-set blonde inquired.

Neither waited for a response as they placed their hands firmly on her shoulders to guide her into the director's chair. Both women leered at her in the mirror, softly brushing fingers through her hair or angling her face. Imogen tried not to squirm at their scrutiny.

"Such cheekbones!" one cooed.

"And virgin hair—my fav!" another gushed.

"Um..." Imogen mumbled. "Who is who?"

The taller woman, with the richest brown eyes Imogen

had ever seen, tittered a high-pitched squeal. "Darling, I'm Lucy. And I am here to save your hair. Great hair days are my specialty!"

"And I'm Mariah," added the younger woman. "You'll look like a whole new person by the time I'm done with you."

Imogen offered them both a weak smile. While she loved all things movies and Hollywood, she was never interested in the cosmetic side of the industry. If her life depended on it, she could not have named a single beauty product, let alone its use. "I'm so glad to have your help."

Lucy, the hair stylist, cackled again. "Oh, darling, nobody says no to Dolian Crawford. Especially when the man has more money than all the gods combined!"

Frowning, Imogen tried not to let guilt make her leave. Wasting money on things like stylists and makeup artists might be normal for a celebrity, but Imogen was as frugal as they came. Poverty taught her that nothing was guaranteed. She never took the bare minimum for granted because it could all disappear in the blink of eye.

Paying a group of specialists an exorbitant amount of money just to help her fix her hair and put on a dress seemed like the pinnacle of excessive waste to Imogen.

"If you don't mind my saying so, you're a little washed out," Mariah commented. Her chubby fingers gripped Imogen's chin, forcing her to turn her head to all angles. "We really need to brighten up your face."

"Oh my God!" Lucy interrupted as she examined the ends of Imogen's thin hair. "When's the last time you had a trim?! This is ghastly!"

Shame flooded Imogen in waves. She tried not to let her

shoulders slump at their critiques—they were professionals, after all—and forced herself to maintain what dignity she could. Besides, if things were going to develop between Dolian and herself, she needed to look the part and adapt to his lifestyle. These things mattered to the fans who would ogle their pictures and scour the internet for information on their personal lives. Imogen would know, she was one of them.

"Just do whatever you need to do," she replied resolutely.

Matching evil grins, not unlike the Grinch's notorious mug shot, greeted her in the mirror.

It took close to two hours for the cosmetic team to be satisfied. Talia, the clothes stylist, joined them around the halfway mark, assuring Imogen that Austin looked very dashing. It was the only kind thing anyone said the entire time.

Lucy and Mariah repeatedly made snide comments and backhanded remarks about so-called shortcomings with Imogen's features. Her skin was too oily, her scalp was too dry, her pointed chin didn't fit with "their vision." It was torture to sit and listen to their critiques. Once Talia joined them, holding up her dress suggestions based on the hair and makeup, Imogen hoped for an ally against the negativity.

However, she was soon disappointed when Talia added to the criticism. Apparently, Imogen was too short, too slight, and had no discernible features whatsoever. Talia grew increasingly frustrated that none of the dress selections would make Imogen stand out. She didn't have the guts to tell the trio that she had no desire to stand out and merely wanted to survive the evening with Dolian.

Finally settling on a simple black silk shift dress, Talia helped slither the smooth material over Imogen's head. The stylists unanimously agreed that Imogen didn't need much in the way of undergarments since she had "no figure to support anyway," but Imogen found the loss to be noticeable. Perhaps she was a prude because she found the lack of bra to be a bit indecent.

When Dolian returned from the bathroom, his hair in a sexy, faux hawk style and guyliner to accentuate his eyes, Imogen bit back the moan that longed to escape. He wore a black tuxedo with a silver shirt, a divergence from the standard that Imogen loved. Life was unfair enough without having gorgeous men like Dolian Crawford walking around out of reach.

Much to her dismay, Imogen was not the only one who noticed. All three stylists collectively swooned, stopping their fluttering the moment he walked in. Their criticisms still rattled in her head. She didn't even want to look Dolian in the eye. She was completely unworthy of him.

"Imogen, what's happened?" he asked, ignoring the trio to round the chair and squat down in front of Imogen. He took both her hands in his and looked up at her, trying to catch her eye.

Imogen glanced at the women behind her, circling like vultures, and refused to meet his gaze. It was enough of a hint that he barked out, "Leave us!" and the women scampered like cockroaches.

As much as she hated it, the tears started to prickle in Imogen's eyes. "They just had some very strong opinions on my flaws," she sighed. There was no point in refusing to tell him because Dolian would bully it out of her anyway. "It's nothing."

"Your flaws?" Dolian repeated incredulously. The grip on her hands tightened slightly. "What flaws?"

Imogen snorted. "Call them back in. They had a list." She flushed with embarrassment.

Sneaking a glance upward, she saw that Dolian was livid. His face turned an angry shade of scarlet and his teeth bared like he wanted to rip out a throat.

"Excuse me," he snarled. Imogen didn't bother to look up as he exited the room to find the three women simpering over him on the other side. Their flattery sounded so vapid that Imogen wanted to vomit.

Whatever Dolian said was too low for her to hear from across the room, but she jumped when he slammed the door with a loud *THWACK*! Rather than returning to her side, he began pacing the room, panting like a bated bull in the ring.

"How dare they treat you like that!" he bellowed. "They don't deserve to breathe the same air as you!"

Imogen remained frozen in place. Movement might stoke the fire, and she had no desire to have his fury directed towards her. Besides, it was a bit over dramatic. Was Imogen upset? Sure. But they were clearly catty, unprofessional women. The solution was to simply not hire them again. Dolian didn't need to be so worked up over something so minor.

The pacing suddenly stopped and Dolian stomped towards her with a menacing scowl. He stopped abruptly at her feet, leaning down as he cupped her face in his hands. "Go take all that shit off your face," he commanded in a voice cut on ice. "I told them to make you look like a Hollywood star, not a Hollywood whore."

Imogen's lower lip trembled. Dolian's words were unnecessarily cruel, but she doubted very much that he would register that message if she tried to deliver it now. Her eyes swam with tears that she blinked away. Slowly, so as not to startle him, Imogen backed away until her butt reached the mirror. Only then did she dare to dart around him into the bathroom, shakily shutting the door behind her.

Her face was ghostly white in the mirror as she leaned over the counter to stare at her reflection. This was not the Dolian she knew. This was the Dolian described on the dark web, prone to fits of rage and violence. It honestly wouldn't have surprised her if he struck something or some*one*.

Hastily, she gathered a white washcloth and doused it with cold water. She had to scrub hard enough that her face turned red, but she managed to get most of the makeup off. The eye makeup was subtle enough that she left most of it on, assuming it was appropriate for whatever function they were attending.

Imogen kept her eyes downcast as she exited the bathroom. Gregory was nowhere to be seen, but Dolian adjusted his bow tie in the mirror. He burst into a wide smile at the sight of her reflection.

"You look beautiful," he assured her.

She wished she could believe him. She wished she could revel in what a spectacular night this was, something any woman would give her right arm for. But the words *Hollywood whore* flashed repeatedly in her mind, and Imogen couldn't make them disappear. Every time she thought she knew Dolian's personality, a new trait emerged. She knew he was an actor, but the constant back and forth gave her whiplash.

"Are you angry with me, sweetheart?" Dolian asked. He crossed the room to her, taking her hands in his own once more.

Keeping her eyes on her feet, Imogen shrugged. "I'm fine. Where are we going?"

Thankfully, the movie star didn't call her out on the abrupt subject change. "The event isn't far from here. Let's find Austin and that social worker, and we can be on our way."

"*That social worker,*" Imogen ground out, "has a name. Don't be dismissive." As soon as the remark left her mouth, she regretted it, bracing herself for the fury that was sure to follow.

Yet Dolian only smiled at her indulgently as he looped her arm through his. "Of course he does." Leading her out of the room, they returned to the living room where Austin and Sully waited. Austin wore a more traditional tuxedo, complete with white bow tie, and did look rather dashing. There was no sign of the stylists. Not that Imogen really expected them to still be there.

Her brother was smiling, however, and that was enough for Imogen to mask her anxiety.

"Look at you, buddy!" she cried. Enveloping Austin in a hug, she swallowed the lump in her throat.

That was easier than swallowing her fear.

EIGHTEEN

The limousine waited for them at the entrance of The Majestic and whisked them away the moment the doors closed. Huxley was already inside, sitting in the passenger cabin this time rather than up with the driver. He shot Sully an appraising look before taking out an iPad and scrolling through it.

Tension filled the air, especially since nobody said a word. While Dolian sighed contentedly next to her, lacing his fingers through hers once more to pull her hand onto his lap, Imogen's stomach twisted in knots. She still had no idea where they were going, and oddly enough, Austin's behavior was rather subdued. Austin wore his emotions right on his sleeve, which Imogen appreciated as a form of communication, but he currently appeared rather forlorn. His shoulders sagged as he sat quietly in his seat. An unusual feat in its own right.

Sully kept glancing back and forth between Imogen and Dolian with a furtive expression that she desperately wanted to inquire about. The first opportunity she had for a quiet conversation in private would be a blessing. Sully had always been the most laidback, casual type of person whenever she observed him at work. That was why Austin loved him so much. Nothing rattled Sully.

Now, however, his stiff back and fidgeting hands suggested something finally nagged underneath his skin. It was almost a relief to know that it wasn't just Imogen. Others noticed the stifling atmosphere.

Imogen turned her attention to the window and realized they were heading into downtown Los Angeles. Traffic was heavy, which was inevitable in L.A., but when they turned onto Sunset Boulevard, Imogen sat up a little straighter. Police were guiding other limousines and impressive vehicles into a processional that led to a red carpet. Paparazzi were everywhere, with camera flashes practically turning the night sky into day. They were at Hollywood Palladium, Imogen realized, a historical venue that hosted parties, ceremonies, and concerts. Imogen had never been inside, but used to love walking by as it was only a block away from the Hollywood Walk of Fame.

Before she had any time to prepare herself or Austin, the limo pulled up to the red carpet and a steward in a suit opened the door. Huxley got out first, pushing back paparazzi that dared to push forward and get a riskier shot. In that moment, Imogen watched as Dolian heaved a huge breath as though bracing himself before plastering a giant smile on his face as he exited the vehicle. He immediately waved at the cheering fans and screaming members of the press, while a jumbotron over the doors of the Palladium showed the live footage of Dolian's entrance. Speakers loudly announced the arrival of the event's host, which Imogen realized was Dolian himself.

All too soon, he turned back and held out a hand for her. Her brain converted to a crash-zoom shot, focusing on each individual face of the paparazzi as Imogen hyperventilated. What if any of them remembered her from the *Agent Reckless* premiere? Were they all judging her again? She wanted to run but she lost use of her legs as the echoes of the photographers' questions sounded like they came from the top of a long well.

"Who is that on your arm, Dolian?"

"How long have you been dating?"

"Is it serious?"

"Dolian, what's your lady's name?"

Dolian wrapped a possessive arm around her waist to draw her closer. It was probably the only reason she was able to stand as her legs still didn't want to cooperate.

There were so *many* of them. Flashing cameras lined both sides of the red carpet, and even though other celebrities still walked, pausing to speak to different media outlets, they all seemed to be zeroed in on her.

Of course they are, Imogen thought. *Dolian Crawford has never attended an event with a date before.*

The only thing that could ever shift her attention was the wailing sound of Austin's distress. She was still blocking the door to the limo and Austin wanted to get out.

"I'm sorry, honey," cooed Imogen. Austin had never been in a crowd or situation like this before and her nurturing instincts wanted to take him away from all the fuss. She pulled away from Dolian to wrap her arm around her brother's shoulders, preparing to shield him from the paparazzi. But to her surprise, Austin smiled and waved at everyone. Several people in the crowd cheered.

"Don't worry, Imogen," Dolian whispered in her ear, his arm sealing around her waist again. "Austin is the man of the hour. I've taken care of everything." Another wide smile stretched across his face as he beamed down at her before turning to wave to the adoring crowds on either side. Austin continued to smile and wave beside them.

Sully brought up the rear as they all slowly made their way up the red carpet. The jumbotron above the entrance changed to a static image welcoming guests to the first ever Austin Reilly Foundation Gala.

Imogen stopped abruptly, not even registering when Sully collided with her and stumbled backward. Pointing up at the screen, she just spewed out on odd assortment of incoherent syllables as Dolian watched her with a bemused expression.

"It's much better that Austin is here tonight," Dolian said quietly in her ear. "I'm glad things happened this way."

Imogen didn't know what to say. Had Dolian seriously named an entire charity after her brother, the most important person in her life? Forget swooning, Imogen was ready to chain herself to him and serve her heart on a solid gold platter. It was easily the most romantic, considerate gesture he could have done, and all doubts as to Dolian's motives and character went out the window.

She always was overly dramatic. Everybody said so, even

when she was a child. Nothing that happened back at the hotel could have been that bad. Shame on her for letting all the fake news from Dylan's dark web get to her. Dolian wasn't a terrible person.

Tearfully, Imogen finally managed to gush, "You're amazing!" in a reverent tone.

Dolian's eyes gleamed. "Anything for you, my sweet. Come. There's so much more in store for you tonight."

Hearing the term of endearment sent sparks of pleasure up her spine. How lucky was she to have someone like Dolian Crawford cherish her?

NINETEEN

"Dolian played a dad so well! You know someone like that has to be a nurturing soul!"
-Helen Langenderfer, The Nocturnal Show

Inside the Palladium, Imogen felt like a princess. White gloved servers in white tuxedo jackets served champagne in crystal flutes. Cascades of glass that resembled icicles hung from the ceiling, interspersed with the long vines of colorful flowers. Imogen had no idea what kind of flowers they were, but they looked exotic to her and filled the air with a rich fragrance. Round tables that seated ten ensconced a gleaming glass dance floor on three sides. A full orchestra filled the stage, playing gentle music that mixed into the background as though it was part of guests' conversations.

There were hundreds of people already mingling and out on the dance floor. Imogen recognized several A-list celebrities, including former costars from Dolian's movies. She tried not to let her jaw drop when she caught sight of the California governor at a table. Everyone in attendance was someone important, and Imogen couldn't imagine how insignificant she must seem to them all. They were all clearly there because of their connection to Dolian, making her wonder what explanation he gave for the new foundation he sponsored.

An area in the back corner of the room had a few other people with Down Syndrome. One of them looked vaguely familiar from the Day Center, and her suspicions were confirmed when Sully raised his hand in greeting. The lighting in that area was far more muted. A small rack held noise canceling headphones. Dry erase boards lined the walls with buckets underneath that Imogen observed a girl drop a marker into. It was meant to be an area for sensitivity so that those in attendance with sensory issues had a safe place.

"You shouldn't drink this on an empty stomach," Dolian warned her as she downed a glass of champagne. "Let's find you some hors d'oeuvres."

Imogen shook her head with a smile. "My stomach is in knots right now. I doubt I could eat anything."

He gave her a furtive look, but nodded. "Would you like to dance?"

Her smile grew wider. "Yes!"

Perhaps it was her imagination, but Imogen's skin warmed as all eyes darted their way when Dolian led her out on the dance floor. A spotlight flooded them as he spun her out before spinning her back into his chest. Dolian's hand was firm in the middle of her back, holding her to him as he twirled them around. Spectators lightly clapped as he dipped her low.

"Everyone's watching us!" She tried not to stare back at

them, but it was unsettling to be the center of such attention.

For his part, Dolian either didn't notice or simply didn't care. He only had eyes for Imogen, his gaze fixated on her face as he effortlessly led them through the dance. "Of course they are." Dolian's voice was confident. "No one can believe how stunningly beautiful my girlfriend is."

Imogen's cheeks burned. "Is that what I am?" she asked incredulously.

The question must have unnerved Dolian because he stopped in the middle of the dance to stare at her. An intensity like she'd seen back at the hotel morphed his eyes into steel. "Yes," seethed Dolian. "You are mine."

An undercurrent to his tone brought an involuntary chill to Imogen's heart. There was a finality to his statement that suggested she had little say in the matter. She blinked away the fear and forced a smile on her face, remembering the night he had planned in her brother's honor.

"I'm almost due for my speech." Dolian grinned at her, showcasing his dimples. The kind of smile that graced all the posters on her wall and always made her heart flutter. And it was meant for *her*.

The music paused and a statuesque woman with dark skin walked to the podium at center stage. She wore a ruby ball gown that glittered under the bright lights.

"Good evening," the woman greeted everyone. "I am Davida Bowles, tonight's Master of Ceremonies, and the director of the California Initiative for Inclusion. When Dolian Crawford contacted me about starting this foundation, I'll admit, I was rather taken aback. But who can say no to a face like that?" She laughed good-naturedly, as did the rest of the crowd, and a spotlight shone on Dolian, who waved in a bemused sort of way to the lookers-on.

Davida continued, "I am so very pleased to welcome everyone to the inaugural Austin Reilly Foundation Gala. Allow me to introduce none other than Dolian Crawford himself, who would like to say a few words about his new organization." With a bright smile, she waved towards Dolian as if to beckon him up the stairs to join her.

Dolian whispered mischievously, "Just wait here!" before dashing up to center stage to a raucous round of applause.

It took several minutes for the room to die down as the celebrities cheered for him. Imogen surged with pride to know someone so beloved considered her worthy enough to be on his arm. Both dimples appeared as he beamed out at her, the lone spotlight tagging her in a beacon this time.

"Ladies and gentlemen, please give the applause for the woman who is deserving of it. May I have the pleasure of introducing Imogen Reilly, the woman who sparked all of this. Her kindness and empathy have always impressed me, and it's an honor to have her as my escort here tonight."

Imogen's skin burned all the way down to her toes as she actively fought the urge to run from the room. All eyes were assessing her, judging her, and she couldn't help but feel an ounce of annoyance at Dolian's choice of words. "Escort" sounded borderline indecent and certainly didn't indicate that there were any feelings between them. It was a loaded term at best, given their company. Many powerful men in the room undoubtedly used escort services to cheat on their wives.

"The Austin Reilly Foundation embodies my personal mission to ensure that the members of the Down Syndrome community have access to resources that facilitate an easier life. It also provides much needed assistance to their caregivers, who are often the silent victims in this community." Dolian's eyes flashed in Imogen's direction. Another round of applause echoed after his speech. "My hope is that with your generous donations tonight, we can provide those with Down Syndrome and their caregivers in Los Angeles County with a 24 hour, state of the art community center that includes medical care, mental health treatment, rehabilitative services, and recreational pursuits."

A large red tapestry hung from the rafters on stage right that now crumpled to the floor to reveal another giant screen. It depicted a blueprint of a four story building with two different wings on either side of a main atrium. An enormous playground, with mobility accessibility for disabled children, was adjacent to the building and surrounded by a circular biking trail. There was also a small pool and splash pad area. It was the perfect set up for those with disabled children who needed a safe place to play and cool off during the long, summer days.

Tears readily streamed down Imogen's cheeks, which she knew would be pointless to stop. The entire endeavor was so overwhelming—more so than anything else Dolian had ever done. There were no articles or reports of him donating anything to charity, let alone starting an entire foundation. Austin would greatly benefit from a community center like this. Hell, so would Imogen. They would always have a place to go and she wouldn't have to worry about time constraints.

She couldn't hear whatever Dolian said to wrap up his speech because she was too lost in thought, but the pounding of applause startled her back into the moment. He gave small smiles and handshakes to everyone who stopped him as he descended the stairs while Davida Bowles returned to the podium to inform everyone of the ways they could donate and what all was still needed.

A gruff finger poked her shoulder and Imogen whirled around to find one of the maître d's giving her an apologetic look. "There's a detective at the door who insists he has to talk to you, Miss Reilly." The man nodded back towards the door as if to emphasize his point.

Her stomach dropped as if she were freefalling off a ledge. Detective Davani was the only police officer she knew, and Imogen wasn't exactly eager to see him again. She didn't want Dolian to see him and recognize him, though, so she quickly made her way to the door without a backward glance.

Davani stood with the same casual swagger as he had during their previous encounters, complete with the jeans and an open button down. The twinkling lights of the décor looked ominous against the gold badge hooked on his belt. His outfit stuck out like a sore thumb against the splendor of the Palladium, and more than one guest watched him with wide eyes.

"What are you doing here?!" Imogen hissed. Noting the bystanders who did nothing to hide their curiosity, she leaned in closer. "I have nothing more to say to you."

Detective Davani grinned. "You're about to have a really long night," he observed nonchalantly.

"Excuse me?" she asked.

A female officer, different from the one who visited her house on the first meeting with the detective, came up behind her and drew Imogen's hands behind her back. The clang of the metal handcuffs hit her ears before her brain registered what was happening.

"You're under arrest," came the detective's response. Only it sounded hollow, like it came from the end of a long tunnel.

Imogen's heartbeat furiously against her chest as it tried to thaw the ice forming in her veins. Oxygen wasn't filling her lungs like it was supposed to and it made her light-headed. "You can't be serious!"

"As a heart attack," Detective Davani replied jovially. Amusement danced in his eyes as though he enjoyed her predicament. Imogen cursed him under her breath as her cheeks heated with shame.

"Get her out of those fucking handcuffs!" Dolian's furious snarl sent a chill down to the marrow in her bones. Seething, he came to stand directly in front of her, blocking the detective from Imogen's sight.

Detective Davani chuckled lightly. "No can do, Mr. Crawford. I've got a warrant for Miss Reilly's arrest. She'll be leaving here with me now."

"Send the warrant to my attorney and we'll get it handled," Dolian argued. "Imogen isn't going anywhere."

Several people were outright staring. Imogen wanted to crawl under a rock and never be seen again because this was mortifying. Strangely, not a single person held up a cell phone or took any photographs, however. Maybe they feared getting on Dolian's bad side. Or maybe guests weren't allowed to have their cell phones on them at the event. Imogen might have slipped past security on that one since she arrived on Dolian's arm.

She peered around Dolian's arms where his fists were

clenched on his hips. The temperature in the room seemed to be rising from the wrath radiating off his person. He started to breathe heavily, labored. It was taking all of his self-control not to snap on the detective.

"No flashy lawyer is gonna get her out of a murder charge." Davani said it in a stage whisper, but he might as well have shouted it from the rafters for the way it made Imogen flinch.

"Whatever her bail is, I'll pay it," gritted out Dolian. "Just take those handcuffs off her."

Davani smiled at Dolian, the air of amusement still playing on his lips. "We haven't set bail yet, but I'll let you know when we do. C'mon, Fullbright." Leaning around Dolian, the detective nodded to the officer behind Imogen, and the female officer jerked Imogen forward.

The last thing Imogen saw from the corner of her eye was Sully's confused gape at the edge of the crowd that gathered. Austin stood beside him, more concerned with pointing out the different decorations as he found them. She didn't have time to ask Sully to take Austin home before the officer pushed her outside and into the waiting police car.

TWENTY

Neither of the officers said anything to Imogen on the way to the police station. The only sound was the chattering of her teeth because of how hard she shook with fear. Getting arrested was by far the worst thing to ever happen to her, and then adding in the murder charge left Imogen on the verge of a full blown panic attack.

The headquarters of the Los Angeles Police Department normally took Imogen's breath away, only now it was for an entirely different reason. In the sinister light lingering just after sunset, all of the windows of the administrative portion of the building now looked foreboding. She never had a reason to go inside before, having never been in any kind of legal trouble. People who lived in her neighborhood still mistrusted the police system, and vigilante justice tended to rule out.

Once inside, Detective Davani read Imogen her full Miranda rights, then took her fingerprints and mug shots. Rather than making her change into the thin cotton shirt and pants that inmates were assigned, the detective brought her a zip up hoodie that smelled faintly of Downey fabric softener and curry. Still, it was soft and clean, a far more welcome alternative, but Imogen couldn't get her mouth to work to thank him. He led her into an interrogation room and didn't bother to hand cuff her to the desk.

"Would you like some coffee? Or water?" he offered.

Nursing the biggest headache of her life, Imogen nodded wearily. "Coffee with cream, if possible," she requested.

Davani turned and nodded towards the glass where she presumed there were other officers waiting before taking a seat across from her. Imogen leaned forward, resting her elbows on the table, and waited.

"This is quite the story," Davani commented offhandedly. "Did you want to make your own headline? Give yourself the 'inside scoop'?" He used finger quotations as he said it. "Because I gotta tell you, Imogen, you don't seem like the type to commit murder."

"That's because I'm not!" she wailed. "I could never hurt anyone!"

The detective nodded. "And what can you offer me by way of an alibi so that I'll believe you?"

Imogen felt exasperated. This was the same conversation they'd had in her apartment. "I already told you, I was home with my brother Austin. I can't leave him home alone because he has Down Syndrome and gets destructive whenever he's unhappy."

"Is that a family trait?" Detective Davani smirked at his own joke. "Why would you want Evette Coleman dead?"

"I didn't! She used to be my idol! I wanted to work on her show, at one point." Exhaustion hit Imogen then. She sank back into her chair and tried to hold back the feeling of defeat.

"Murder is a good way to ensure there's an opening," he deadpanned.

The door opened and the female officer, Fullbright, brought in a paper cup of coffee with a lid. She glared at Imogen as she placed the cup at Davani's elbow before swiftly exiting the room. Sliding the cup towards her, Davani leaned back in his own seat before continuing.

"So, it turns out that you've left Austin alone at night before," he said. "Co-workers of your mom's said she's had to call off multiple times because you weren't home. Her attendance at her night job is actually so bad that she's on the verge of losing it."

This was revelatory to Imogen, who had no idea her mother missed so much work. She was home so little that her daughter never would have known Sylvia struggled with attendance. Where was her mom going if she wasn't at work?

"I've never seen my mother miss work," Imogen whispered reproachfully. The detective wanted to wind her up and he was succeeding. "We can barely keep the lights on. She wouldn't risk losing that paycheck."

He nodded in agreement. "Which makes it all the more concerning that your mom has had to leave so many times.

Why would a woman do that if her daughter was actually providing the care she was *paid* to provide?"

Imogen's cheeks burned. "I've never seen a penny of that money." The admission tasted like ash in her mouth. "My mother controls all our finances. She gives me a bit of cash here and there to get by."

Davani's hard eyes glinted over with something akin to pity. He regarded her for a moment before clearing his throat. "Are you telling me your mother and her coworkers are lying about her attendance issue?"

Imogen sighed. "I'm telling you I wouldn't know which was the lie or the truth in that scenario. I have no idea what money is in the bank or where my mom is. She's never home, so if she says she's missing shifts at the nursing home, it is *not* because of me or Austin." The injustice of it all stung because Sylvia had never put their needs above her jobs before. Even on days when Imogen could barely get out of bed from the flu, she had to care for Austin.

Pausing, Davani switched tactics. "Let's go over that whole night again," he suggested. "How did you find yourself at the *Agent Reckless* premiere in the first place?"

"I won the contest." Bitterness crept into her tone. While Imogen could not have been more grateful to meet Dolian, attending a movie premiere no longer impressed her like it once had. The price of admission was too high if it landed Imogen in prison.

His eyebrows furrowed. "What contest?"

She never got a chance to answer because the door burst open, smacking loudly into the wall to announce Dolian's entrance.

"That's enough!" he shouted. "Imogen won't be

answering anymore questions." A seedy looking man in a three piece black suit swept into the room, clutching a leather briefcase. Even though they were indoors at night, a large pair of sunglasses covered most of his face.

"I am Miss Reilly's attorney," the man said in a gruff voice. He sounded as though he chain smoked three packs a day. "I've already spoken to a judge and given the circumstances, she is free to go."

Detective Davani sprung from his seat in outrage. "What circumstances?! Who are you?"

Rather than answer him, the man pulled a stapled stack of papers from his briefcase and shoved them at the detective. Davani glanced at them, and his face contorted in shock. "There's been another murder? How do we know this is even related to the Reilly case?"

Dolian's face was unreadable as he replied, "Because it was the caregiver assigned to her brother tonight, a Charles Sullivan, otherwise known as Sully."

Imogen's heart bottomed out as she sank to the ground with a wail. Poor Sully. He was the kindest, most gentle hearted man. Who could do something so evil to someone so pure?

She suddenly remembered the way he looked in the limousine on the way to the gala. Sully wanted to tell her something then, Imogen was sure of it. And now she would never get the chance to ask him.

"So as you can see, you need to change the angle of your investigation!" Dolian growled. "Imogen is the victim, not the perpetrator!"

When he said it, fear finally kicked in. This was someone Imogen had known for almost a year and never had a cross encounter. Whoever killed Sully struck a lot closer to home than Evette Coleman and Jesse Ramirez. Negative interactions with them were totally eclipsed by the murder of someone close to her. Could the murderer actually have Imogen in their sights?

"What about Austin?" Imogen sobbed. Guilt, fear, and despair created a tornado inside her. "Where is he?"

"Back at the hotel with another caregiver. I'll explain in the car." Still, Dolian did not look at her, but kept his eyes trained on Davani.

"We'll be leaving now," the attorney announced again. He held out a business card to the detective. "Contact me before you contact Miss Reilly again. I will handle all of her communication going forward."

In a display of gallant concern, Dolian wrapped a protective arm around Imogen's shoulders to lead her from the room. Truthfully, tears were running so fat and thick down her face, she couldn't see anything in front of her anyway. A coldness seeped into her bones. And while Imogen was grateful for Dolian's assistance, none of it brought her any comfort at the moment. Sully, one of her brother's favorite people in the world, had been murdered.

"How did this even happen?" wailed Imogen as soon as the car doors shut behind them. Dolian's usual driver slid in behind the steering wheel after closing the door. "Sully was at the gala with you! I saw him when I was getting arrested!"

"Shh!" Dolian coddled, pulling Imogen into his arms and stroking her hair. "You have to settle your nerves and avoid going into shock. I don't want to take you to a hospital, my sweet!"

Anger flashed across Imogen's face. "I am NOT going into

shock, Dolian! What happened to Sully? Who is that attorney?"

He withdrew his arms, caging her in against the seat instead. "All that matters is you and Austin are both fine." There was an edge to his voice that made Imogen's skin break out in goosebumps.

"And I'm Saul Whitehouse, Mr. Crawford's attorney," the attorney offered, holding out a hand to shake hers. "Mr. Crawford keeps an active retainer on file to keep my services on standby. I'll be handling your case, at his request. Although the charges will be formally dropped first thing tomorrow," he added.

Imogen blinked as she processed that information. "You keep an attorney on standby?"

Saul shrugged. "It's pretty standard for celebrities, Miss Reilly. Don't read too much into it. However, I do have to advise you both to stay away from one another for a little bit." He grimaced as if bracing himself.

And with good reason. Dolian's hackles rose like he was prepared to rip the man's head off inside the SUV. "Excuse me?" he thundered.

"Dolian, the media storm that's about to surround this case will destroy your career," Saul warned. "This is going to be headline news for a long time, and while we know Imogen is innocent, the public's opinion won't be so cut and dry. They'll be out for blood. Her blood isn't nearly as important to them as yours."

It mimicked the Contact's warnings so closely that Imogen angled her head to look more closely at him. The large sunglasses remained on inside the car, further obscuring his face in the dark light.

"Then I'll have my usual media clean up crew fix it!" snapped Dolian. If looks could kill, the attorney would be reduced to a pile of ash.

A media clean up crew? Imogen thought back to Dylan's explanation of Dolian's misdeeds only appearing on the dark web where they couldn't be repressed. Maybe there was some truth to that story.

"Thank you so much for representing me," Imogen said quietly. Her soft voice made Dolian instantly melt, the tension draining from his body. "Please let me know how much your retainer fee is so that I can pay you myself."

Saul snorted. "My retainer is a minimum of $250,000."

Mouth flapping like a goldfish, Imogen sputtered. How could someone sleep at night while charging people those prices?

"I'm covering the costs, Imogen," Dolian insisted firmly.

As much as she wanted to argue, there was no way she could come up with that kind of money. Bleakly, Imogen nodded in agreement.

The vehicle pulled up to a tall office building in the business district of downtown Los Angeles and stopped at the door.

"This is me," said Saul. "Remember what I said, Dolian. Keep your distance. Don't speak to any media outlets. Just let us handle it. For your own sake." As Dolian's driver opened the door for him, Saul gave Imogen a small nod and left.

But Imogen wasn't about to be deterred. She knew Dolian wanted to commiserate over the attorney's advice while that was the last thing Imogen cared about.

"What happened to Sully?" she begged. "Please! I need to know."

The actor's face was as hard as stone when he replied, "Someone strangled him in the alleyway behind the Palladium."

Imogen gasped. Such a violent end for such a soft-hearted person. "Why was he back there to begin with?"

Dolian shrugged as if it meant nothing to him. Which, Imogen realized, it didn't. He didn't have a past history with Sully like she did. His death couldn't rattle Dolian.

"How is Austin? Did anyone explain it to him?" Imogen felt like she was going to vomit from the image of a distraught Austin in her head.

"Huxley is with him." As if that would make her feel any better. Imogen didn't like Huxley much more than she liked Saul.

When she opened her mouth to ask another question, Dolian held up a hand to stop her. "Let's let the professionals do their jobs to investigate what happened. I'm sure Austin is eagerly awaiting your arrival back at The Majestic."

Imogen recognized the attempt to silence her, but allowed Dolian to do so. There was no point in peppering him with questions when any one of them might set off his volatile temper. She sank back into the seat, craning her neck back to stare at the ceiling. Something about the entire situation felt off. Sully wouldn't hurt a fly. No one could possibly have a motive to kill him specifically, and there were plenty of other people at the gala who presented just as low a risk as him. More importantly, his murder indicated it was someone who was *at* the party, which was a far more troublesome realization.

And Imogen knew exactly who would have the answers she needed.

TWENTY-ONE

"Working with Dolian Crawford is a challenge in and of itself. You have to rise in your craft so that your greatness matches his."
-Peter Ferguson, director

It felt like days passed by the time Austin and Imogen finally made it back to their apartment. Upon arriving at The Majestic, she found her brother loudly pounding his fists against the wall in a bedroom where he had been closed in by himself. An irritated looking Huxley stood outside the door and cast a scathing look in her brother's direction when Imogen rushed inside. Austin was just as distraught as she imagined because he had no concept of death or loss, so having Sully there and gone in so short a time was impossible for him to rationalize.

Dolian shattered a China vase against the wall when Imogen said she wanted to follow Saul's advice and keep their distance from one another for the next few days. Steam was practically billowing out his ears as he frantically begged Imogen to change her mind.

"I can control the news outlets!" insisted Dolian. "We don't need to worry about them!"

As much as it crushed her to hear the desperation in his voice, Imogen remained firm. She was not a celebrity and there was very little chance of her blog ever being taken seriously at this point if she continued to gallivant around with the world's biggest movie star in the wake of a murder scandal.

"This is for the best," Imogen insisted.

She expected a romantic plea like the speech he delivered in *Christopher's Romp*. Or a heartfelt dialogue about how their love could overcome any obstacle like his character in *Our Gentleman Callers*. Really, anything dramatic wouldn't have surprised her.

But instead, Dolian Crawford morphed into something darker than Imogen recognized. He had only played a villain in one film, so perhaps it just wasn't naturally in his repertoire, but Dolian's eyes were nearly black in their anger. Tension lined his jaw, braced his shoulders, and stiffened his back. Imogen started to quiver under the intensity of his glare.

"You will regret this," vowed Dolian.

The SUV came to an abrupt halt next to a bus stop in the Valley and Huxley opened the door to let Imogen and Austin out.

"A-are you serious?" Imogen's eyes threatened to pop. She couldn't move, she was so stunned at the venom in his words.

Dolian refused to look at her. His eyes stayed pinned on

the window just over her shoulder, the scowl still marring his perfect face.

Rapidly, she blinked away tears and latched onto Austin's hand to pull him out after her. It started to rain, but whether it was intentional or purely coincidental, there was a cover over the bus stop. This wasn't along their usual route, so Imogen prayed it wouldn't take them several hours to get home.

Huxley glared at her as well before returning to the vehicle.

"Well, Austin, I guess it's just you and me," she said lightly. Taking him by the hand, she led him to the bench under the bus stop awning and sat down. For once Austin sat down beside her and leaned his head on her shoulder. A heavy sigh escaped his lips that Imogen couldn't help but echo.

"I know, buddy," she said. "Today has been rough all around."

The rain pounded hard on the pavement, spraying her dress and ricocheting off the metal roof. Anything that drowned out her feelings was a welcome reprieve. Too much had happened in such a short amount of time, and she wasn't ready to process it. Exhaustion wanted to pull her under. Imogen didn't care if she needed to sleep in bed with Austin that night so long as she got to sleep soon.

Poor Sully. He hadn't deserved to die. Especially frightened and in pain while attending a charity gala. Imogen didn't know if he had any family, but she felt the bile rise in her throat to picture horrified expressions of disbelief upon receiving the news of his murder. Not to mention, she needed a way to explain the loss to Austin. Sully was the one who could always calm him down at the Day Center. Would it be harder for him to attend now if Sully wasn't there to keep the peace?

Austin remained just as quiet and subdued on the bus ride home. Imogen reasoned that they both were probably dealing with sensory overload. Their five floor walk up had never been so welcoming before. She didn't protest when Austin stripped down to his boxers and crawled immediately into bed without brushing his teeth or putting his clothes in the hamper.

But after Imogen finished her own nightly routine and changed into her preferred yoga pants and tank top combo, her obsession reared its ugly head. She had never gone to bed in the past eight years without going through her Dolian Crawford scrapbook. Her brain didn't want to sleep until her compulsion was satisfied.

After tossing and turning for close to thirty minutes, Imogen gave in. Photograph after photograph of Dolian's sexy smolder, of him in a wet shirt next to a pool, of him leaning against a muscle car. That was one of her favorite shoots because it tied into his Formula 1 movie where he played a racecar driver. It was the first film where Dolian really got to show off his range as an actor.

And yet, now that she knew him more intimately, something about all of the photographs felt off. Dolian was no longer as charming or handsome as he used to be. Imogen could tell that his smile never fully extended to his eyes, making them all an imitation of an emotion she didn't believe him capable of feeling.

The buzz of her cell phone caused Imogen to jump.

The Contact. He would help her sort through the mess.

she typed back.

Comfort from the assurance that the Contact would resolve everything finally allowed Imogen to drift off to sleep. All would be well with his help.

TWENTY-TWO

"Dolian Crawford is one actor I'll never work with again. He's so good that he makes me look bad!"
-TJ Simmons, Our Gentleman Callers *co-star*

Sylvia shook Imogen awake the next morning and slapped a newspaper onto the nightstand beside her with a hiss.

"Is there something you'd like to tell me?" her mother seethed.

Groggily, Imogen blinked down at the enormous headline.

DOLIAN CRAWFORD'S GIRLFRIEND ARRESTED

Imogen groaned as she rubbed her eyes. "I already have a lawyer, Mom. It's all gonna blow over."

"Blow over?" Sylvia repeated. "BLOW OVER? That's the only thing you have to say for yourself after I show you a newspaper with your picture in it that says you've been charged and arrested for MURDER?!" She snorted in disgust.

The digital alarm clock on the dresser said it was only six A.M., but Imogen threw off the blankets anyway. Her mother wouldn't hear a word Imogen had to say so she might as well get up and make some coffee. With a heavy sigh, Imogen pulled on a robe and flip flops, piling her hair into a messy bun on top of her head as she shuffled into the kitchen. Sylvia followed.

"I told you that man was bad news! Look at what he's costing you, Imogen!" The newspaper crinkled in Sylvia's hand as she held it up for her daughter to look at again. "What if you go to prison, huh? What will happen to your brother? To me? D'you think I want to see my only daughter behind bars?!"

"MOTHER!" Imogen finally snapped. "There was another murder at the gala while I was in custody, so all charges against me are being dropped. They already know I didn't do it."

Sylvia frantically flipped through the newspaper as if fact checking her daughter's explanation. "There's nothing in here about another murder!" she countered. "Was it somebody famous?"

At this question, Imogen's stomach bottomed out. No, Sully wasn't famous, but he was somebody very important to Austin. It was unlikely that Sylvia would even remember Sully if Imogen mentioned his name. In fact, she couldn't recall them ever meeting.

Even now, despite the coldness with which Dolian dismissed her, Imogen wanted to shield him from her mother's hatred. Sylvia would undoubtedly blame the movie star if she knew someone so close to their family had been murdered at an event Dolian sponsored. Bending the truth would be best.

"It hasn't made the news yet." Imogen swallowed thickly. "He was a nobody."

The lie tasted sour in her mouth.

"Then how do they know the murder is related?" Sylvia demanded.

Imogen diverted her gaze so that the tears in her eyes didn't betray her true feelings. "He was working at the gala Dolian and I attended."

A loud *harumph!* followed. Sylvia crossed her arms over her chest while jutting out a hip. "Oh, I read all about that! How a bunch of celebrities came to throw money at a charity named after MY son! If Dolian really cared about Austin, I would have been invited, too!"

Only Imogen could have detected the jealousy in her mother's tone.

"Mom, you haven't exactly been very nice to him! Why would he include you in something special he tried to do for me?"

The scent of fresh coffee filled the air as the old Coffeemate kicked in. Just smelling it made Imogen feel better. She ignored the hostility rolling off her mother as she prepared a few slices of toast to go along with it.

"When I told you to get a job, Imogen, I expected you to do something respectable. I'd rather you do anything else."

Exasperated, Imogen slammed down the plate on the rickety table, glaring at her mother. "What am I doing that's so disrespectful, Mom? Please, enlighten me!"

Fury burned in Sylvia's eyes as she hissed, "There's nothing respectful about being a worthless man's whore!"

Pain so acute it might as well be delivered by a blow to

the gut poured into Imogen's heart. She had never heard something so vile cross her mother's lips. Long gone were the dreams of a reconciliation where Imogen and Sylvia grew closer and loved one another as mother-daughter pairs usually did.

Imogen recoiled from the ugly words, gaping at her mother in silent horror. "That was a terrible thing to say," she scolded.

There wasn't a morsel of regret in Sylvia's expression. "The truth is hard to hear. You're so brainwashed by that asshole that you genuinely can't see all the problems he's created for us. I deserve better than this from you, Imogen."

She rolled her eyes. "Why? Because of all you've done for me?" Imogen made air quotes with her fingers.

But Sylvia's eyes filled with tears. "Yes," she said simply. The fight went out in her, and she headed for the bathroom, tossing the newspaper on the table as she went. The table was so small that it landed on Imogen's toast. Not that it mattered. She no longer had an appetite.

Picking up the paper, she perused the rest of the article. Celebrity guests were mentioned more than Imogen, and the article focused more on Dolian's lack of dating history than her arrest. She was glad to see the report that the gala raised $2.6 million towards the Down Syndrome Community Center, but now that things were so fractured between her and Dolian, would he even come through with it?

Unbidden sobs worked their way up Imogen's throat, and she stuffed a fist in her mouth to try and muffle the sound. Austin didn't deserve to see her like this. She had finally managed to get herself in such a pickle that even the Contact would probably turn on her. Imogen dreaded their impending call that afternoon—assuming she could find a way to sneak out of the house now that her mother was in such a vile mood.

Her phone began to ring in her robe pocket and Imogen answered automatically without bothering to wipe the tears from her face. It was a FaceTime call…*from Dolian!*

"No, Imogen, why are you crying?!" Dolian looked to be on a private plane given the white leather and rich paneling behind him. He stared at her with concern, brows furrowing into a crease on his forehead. "Please don't cry, sweetheart! I'm so, so sorry about how I acted yesterday! It was wrong on a number of levels."

The apology only made Imogen cry harder. She was desperate to believe him, to have some kind of proof to offer her mother that she and Dolian had a real relationship and that this wasn't all in her head.

"My mom called me some really nasty things!" admitted Imogen with a sharp intake of breath. Guilt like she was tattling to a principal started to form in her heart, but she brushed the feelings away. "She said you're gonna ruin everything for us!"

Although his expression softened, there was a glint of malice to his eyes that Imogen didn't like. "I am only going to make everything better," Dolian promised passionately. "For you and for us. I—I think I'm falling in love with you, Imogen."

Her mouth fell open in surprise before she had a chance to school her features. "Are you sure?" she finally whispered. A faint hope slowly began to grow inside her as she accepted the words she always dreamed of hearing fall from Dolian's lips.

He laughed at her incredulity. "Of course. I've never felt anything like this before. All my thoughts, day and night... they're of you. I just want to be with you all the time. Please say you forgive me. That you feel this, too."

Imogen had waited for this moment nearly half her life. Dolian Crawford, her own spicy version of Prince Charming, loved her. The realization barreled into her, making her cry all over again.

"Oh, Dolian," Imogen gushed. "I love you, too!"

"Please tell me you're not talking to that monster right now, Imogen!" Sylvia hovered in the doorway, face aghast.

"Mom, you don't understand," Imogen argued. "Dolian loves me and—"

Sylvia barked out a harsh laugh. "How could he love you when he barely even knows you? Come on, you used to be smart!"

A quick glance at the phone confirmed that Dolian could hear everything Sylvia said...and didn't like it one bit.

"Get off that phone, NOW!" her mother shouted, waving her arms as if to knock the phone from Imogen's grasp. "You're not gonna talk to this man if you live under MY roof!"

"I'm sorry, Dolian, I have to—"

With one fail swoop, the iPhone went flying. Sylvia glared at it as if it were a snake that made its way into her kitchen.

"...go," finished Imogen with a whisper.

There was a pregnant pause wrought with tension. Her mother panted in her fury, sending trembles down Imogen's spine. Yet Imogen meant what she said. She loved Dolian. Always had. And she couldn't believe that Sylvia actually planned to take that away from her.

"Do you seriously want to kick me out?" Imogen asked with a whisper. What had always been an empty threat now sounded like an explicit command.

Sylvia shook her head. "I don't want to, but you're forcing my hand. That man is trouble with a capital T. The law is not on your side with this, Imogen, no matter who your attorney is. Do you think they're going to pin this on Dolian, the international megastar who has millions of fans to rally around him? Or the little nobody from the streets of Compton? The system is designed to work against you."

Her speech was so eerily similar to what the Contact said that Imogen paused.

A lone tear rolled down Sylvia's cheek. "I'm scared for you, Imogen," she admitted.

Enveloping her mother in a hug, she nodded into her shoulder. "I'm scared, too. But Dolian makes me happy. Why can't I have someone who makes me smile instead of feeling scared?"

Sylvia held her for a long time before she answered. "Because a mother's job is to warn your child when they can't see the danger right in front of them. And right now, you're not seeing it, honey."

A sense of loss followed. At one point in her life, Imogen would have given anything for her mother to say something like that. She often felt more like a live in babysitter than a family member, and she could count on one hand the number of times her mother ever used the words 'I love you.' And while she knew that Sylvia's heart was in the right place, Dolian's love appealed far more. He existed in every fantasy Imogen ever dared to dream.

As long as her mother didn't know about their relationship, they could continue to coexist in the tiny apartment like they always had. Sylvia was there so infrequently that it hardly made a difference anyway. Until Imogen sealed the deal with one of the sponsor opportunities with her blog, Austin needed to stay here, and there was no way Imogen would move out of this apartment without him. She was sure that if she asked Dolian, he would pay for a small house for Imogen and Austin to live in on their own—or better yet, allow the two of them to move in. But that was a conversation best in person.

Imogen pulled away from the embrace and didn't meet her mother's eyes when she nodded. "I understand, Mom. I'll be careful." That was as much of a promise as she could make.

Austin shuffled into the kitchen then, diverting both of their attentions. As Imogen went through the rest of the morning routine and got the apartment clean, her mom's concern rattled in her head. Dylan, the Contact, now her mother—nobody believed Dolian was a good person, or that their love was real.

Why did his fame have to change the way he and Imogen felt about one another? Being in a relationship with Dolian Crawford was everything she had ever hoped for. Someday Netflix or Prime or one of those streaming services would make a documentary about their love story, Imogen could already picture it. She would wind up a household name in her own right, like Priscilla Presley or Kevin Federline, just because she was a "normal" person who married a celebrity.

It was like her mother just didn't want Imogen to be happy.

Thankfully, Sylvia was only home long enough to sleep for

a couple hours before heading downstairs to work at the convenience store. Austin wasn't his usual, lively self, and although Imogen knew he didn't know that Sully died, there was no other explanation for his muted behavior. When she suggested that they head to the library before heading over to The Majestic, Austin merely shook his head. He was content to color in one of his many coloring books at the kitchen table while Imogen scrubbed the kitchen.

Imogen didn't dare check her phone after the call with Dolian ended on such a bad note. With his hotheaded temperament, he was liable to demand she get on a plane and meet him at some remote location while he filmed. And because she was still so in love, and awestruck with the fact that he returned the sentiment, she would likely agree.

She did, however, check her blog, and promptly fell out of her chair. Site views were up over 400% as close to 1.4 million people now read her last article. There were thousands of comments calling for more dirt on the Oscar winner, questions about their relationship, and more often than not, death threat after death threat from jealous fangirls who wanted Dolian for themselves.

"Well you can't have him!" Imogen muttered hotly. Still, there were so many new subscribers that she would actually receive an engagement bonus check from the blog host, something Imogen had never achieved before. There were also hundreds of emails about sponsorship opportunities!

Writing another blog post became her top priority. Saul advised her to lay low, but that was easy for him to say when he could earn a paycheck while staying under the radar. If sharing details about her relationship with Dolian was the only way to keep her views high, what else was she to do?

Life With Dolian Crawford

Nobody suspected that my last post would turn into such a media storm, least of all me. Life's funny that way sometimes, isn't it? Interviewing Dolian Crawford was an exclusive that every journalist worth their salt would kill for—and I didn't even need a body count to do it!

While my previous post about Dolian felt true at the time, I must now admit that my opinion of him has changed entirely. He is an old-soul, someone kind and wonderful, who loves with his whole heart. Life can be lonely, even when people surround you constantly, and I think we as fans tend to forget the human being behind the celebrity.

I deeply regret writing anything that hurt Dolian Crawford. I can admit that.

Many of you have speculated as to the status of our relationship, if there even is a relationship to speculate on, and I'm sorry to say, but you'll leave disappointed. Whatever happens between the actor and myself is entirely our business. We are both entitled to our privacy— Lord knows Dolian gets so little of it!—and quite frankly, I started this blog to share my love of all things Hollywood, not to become gossip fodder for crazed fans.

Tune in for my next blog about the inaugural Austin Reilly Foundation gala. The celebrity guest list will shock you!

Rereading the article, Imogen nodded in satisfaction. It was just enough to whet their appetite without confirming or denying anything. Until she had confirmation from Dolian that he wanted them to announce their relationship (a thought that had Imogen trembling with anxiety), it was best to leave everything open to interpretation. It sounded far more like an adult relationship that way.

She clicked 'submit' before she could overthink it.

"C'mon, Austin," she said. "Let's get ready to head out for the day."

TWENTY-THREE

"Dolian Crawford could not be reached for a comment at this time."
-Derek Federman, ABC News anchor

"I don't know why you're acting like you want my help," the Contact drawled, his exhale long and breathy as if he were actively smoking a cigarette. "You're clearly just going to do whatever the hell you want."

Imogen shifted the weight to her other foot, keeping a close eye on Austin at the table beside her. When they approached The Majestic on the way there, he had gone into a nuclear meltdown. It escalated to the point where he started slapping himself as a way to stim. The behavior was so out of the ordinary for him that Imogen started to cry.

"Please, buddy, everything is okay! I promise!" She had choked back her sobs and wrapped her arms around her brother, pinning his arms to his sides, unwilling to let go. He calmed enough after that that she managed to get him inside, but now he was eating his way through a large banana split. Imogen dreaded to think what the bill would be for such an ostentatious dessert. Maybe she could have it charged to Dolian since he owned the hotel.

"I didn't kill anyone, and I certainly haven't done anything wrong!" Huffing in annoyance, Imogen turned back to the phone call.

The Contact proved to be just as awful about the entire thing as Imogen imagined he would be. He strongly discouraged her from using Dolian's attorney, claiming that if anything went south between her and Dolian, the attorney would roll over on her faster than she could blink. Any insistence that they were in a committed relationship was met with a scoff.

"Trust me, I know Dolian's type," the Contact replied. "He's using you. Get out now while you still can."

She rolled her eyes, grateful that he couldn't see her. "No, he isn't. We're in this for the long haul. Trust me, I'm never letting him go."

There was a pause before the Contact spoke again. "Then why are you coming to me for damage control?"

Imogen considered the question. Why *was* she going to him? What did she honestly expect him to do for her now? As long as Dolian loved her, everything would be fine.

"I guess...this is good-bye," she finally acknowledged. Just saying it out loud made a weight lift off her chest.

He snorted. "No, Glenda, it isn't. You owe me, remember?" There was a condescension in his tone that grated her nerves.

"I'm pretty sure that none of my success has anything to do with you," countered Imogen. "None of your 'leads' really did anything for me. I didn't have anything until he came into the picture."

The sharp intake of breath made her brace for impact. "You," the Contact sneered, "are like a lost, little puppy. Always expecting somebody else to take care of you and do everything for you. You were nothing before Dolian Crawford and you'll be nothing again as soon as he's through with you. Just a pathetic, worthless piece of trash. That's why nobody will come looking for you when I put you in the dumpster where you belong."

A loud click before the dial tone indicated that the call ended, but Imogen found it difficult to breathe. Not only were his accusations the perfect way to bring out her insecurities, but the threat was as blatant as they come. The Contact meant to hurt her. Maybe even worse.

And as her eyes pirouetted to Austin, her sweet, innocent brother, happily eating ice cream without any thought of the dangers that might await them both, Imogen knew she needed to protect him at all costs.

She hung up the receiver and scrambled to look through her purse for the business card Detective Davani gave her. This was definitely the kind of thing she needed to report.

"Davani here," he greeted on the first ring.

"U-um, sir? This is Imogen Reilly," she sputtered.

The detective let out a low whistle. "Imogen Reilly, you're the last person I expected to hear from. Shouldn't you be out looking for your next victim?"

Squeezing her eyes shut as if it would shield her, Imogen whispered, "I think someone is going to hurt me."

There was a creak in the background, like the detective was adjusting his position in an office chair. "You think someone is going to hurt you? Could it be the same person who murdered Charles Sullivan last night?"

When she didn't answer, he asked urgently, "Where are you?"

"At The Majestic hotel."

"Can you get over to The Farmer's Market?"

Imogen swallowed thickly and nodded before remembering he couldn't see her. "Yes. It's not that far."

"I'll meet you there," Detective Davani offered. "Be careful and keep your eyes open."

Rather than respond, Imogen slid the receiver back into place. "C'mon, Austin, we have to go."

A waiter materialized, a patronizing smile decorating his face. "And are we ready for the bill, ma'am?" He held out a black leather folder with a slip of paper sticking out from the top.

Imogen went to great lengths to hide her appearance again, tucking her hair into another wide brimmed hat and donning oversize sunglasses. Another baggy shirt hid her figure. So she was surprised when she pulled her sunglasses off to read the receipt and watched the man take a half step back in shock.

"Miss Reilly, I'm so sorry," the waiter crooned. "Of course there's no bill for you. My sincerest apologies, ma'am." And off he scurried like a rat entering the sewers.

One person could easily turn into one hundred. She shoved the sunglasses back on rather than risk anyone else recognizing her. Hastily, Imogen grabbed Austin's hand and pulled him out of the booth so they could get out of there before Dolian had time to arrive. She wasn't sure if he was still tracking her location with her cell phone, but she also didn't want to find out. Like the coward she was, Imogen wasn't ready to face him after their disastrous phone call.

They didn't have money for a taxi, but taking the bus could extend their trip by an extra hour or two, depending on how bad the traffic was. It might be several blocks, but it was better for them to walk. Imogen held firmly to Austin's hand as he tried to dart into shop after shop to chase whatever caught his attention.His impulsivity was in full swing today and she had enough problems without losing Austin in a crowd.

On the way, she continued to mull over the Contact's visceral response. Baiting him the way she had was the wrong choice, Imogen knew that now, but in the heat of the moment, she had only wanted to prove a point. Was that how crimes of passion started? Did egging him on make her at fault?

At one point there was a man on the other side of the road who appeared to be trailing her. He walked with his head turned in her direction, not paying any mind to the other pedestrians in his way. She couldn't be sure from so far away, but she almost thought the man resembled Huxley. None of Huxley's features were very discernible other than his facial scars, however, and with the foot traffic on a beautiful day in L.A. along with all the cars passing by, it was difficult to be sure. Imogen had to focus more on Austin than anything. When they stopped at an intersection, waiting to cross, she tried to get a better look across the street, blocking the sun in her eyes with her hand.

The man was gone.

Had Imogen imagined him? It couldn't be Huxley because he only went where Dolian went, and there was no way

Dolian could walk down a busy street like this without paparazzi and fans circling him like vultures. An unsettling feeling of being watched plagued her, but she shook it off to focus on Austin.

Detective Davani waited for them at the entrance to the Farmer's Market. It was a popular hangout spot in Los Angeles, filled with vendors who sold overpriced fruits, vegetables, and other handmade goods that all claimed to be organic, holistically, eco-sustainably produced, and whatever other buzzwords they thought justified the twelve dollar price tag for a single tomato. It was hit or miss whether or not Austin would be overwhelmed, but there weren't many people out shopping that day.

She nodded at Davani in greeting.

"Hey, man!" The detective held up a hand to Austin for a high five, which her brother enthusiastically delivered. "Hello, Ms. Reilly."

"Please, just call me Imogen." Gesturing toward Austin, who was already darting towards a vendor with stained glass windchimes, she added, "And try to keep up. He's not going to make this easy on us."

After a few minutes of watching Austin examine the glass, Davani finally asked, "Is this on or off the record, Imogen?"

She glanced around uncomfortably. Nobody even looked their way, and yet the hairs on the back of her neck continued to stand on end. Dolian would be furious if he saw her here with the detective. But clearly Dolian couldn't always be around to protect her. Especially if Imogen kept secrets like the Contact from him.

"Off the record," she decided in a quiet voice. "I've been

getting the content for my gossip blog from an anonymous source for a couple years now. I simply call him 'The Contact.' When I tried to part ways with him just now, he threatened me."

They walked for a bit in silence as Austin moved onto the next vendor that caught his eye, someone who made small toys out of wood. There were a handful of Grecian computer puzzles on display that her brother immediately tried to solve.

"Have you ever met him in person?" Davani inquired.

She shook her head.

"Was it all digital?"

Imogen grimaced before launching into the story of how she came to rely on the Contact after that fateful phone call at The Majestic. Saying it out loud only made her realize how foolish she sounded, giving a complete stranger such sway over her.

The detective didn't appear to judge her, at least. Davani listened intently, keeping his eyes glued to Austin rather than Imogen. When she finished, Davani frowned. "So you only ever spoke to him in person at the hotel?"

"Yes," agreed Imogen. "Calls never went through when I tried to reach him with the number we used for texting."

"And Dolian Crawford owns The Majestic..." Davani's voice trailed off as he finally turned to look at her.

Until now, those two points never connected in Imogen's brain. The old payphones never rang any other time. They were more of a decoration to add to the old Hollywood aesthetic than anything else. Even the employees hadn't so much as second glanced when Imogen answered the phone.

"But it couldn't be Dolian! The Contact has been trying to convince me to leave Dolian alone!"

He shrugged. "I never said it was Crawford."

"Then what are you saying, Detective?"

Her skin grew clammy as Davani replied, "I'm saying that I don't work in a field where I believe in coincidences. There's a reason this so-called 'Contact' would only speak to you on the phone at that hotel."

"So what do I do?" Imogen hated how small and pathetic her voice sounded, like the very child the Contact accused her of being.

Davani grinned. "Officially, I can only advise you to let the police do their jobs. Turn in all of the information you have on this Contact guy and let them investigate. But unofficially," the detective leaned in so that his voice was barely above a whisper, "I would suggest you start using some of your journalistic skills and do some digging. Your name might be cleared for murder right now, Imogen, but a high profile case like Evette Coleman's is gonna demand blood for blood. Sounds like the Contact has the power and the means to make that blood yours."

TWENTY-FOUR

"I am Dolian Crawford's biggest fan! I even got his face tattooed on my arm—look!"
-fan outside the 2019 Emmy Awards

Imogen's insides were so twisted in knots by the time she got home that she wanted to pop an Imodium and then go to bed. Davani's summation of her predicament was like having a cooler of ice water dumped over her head—Imogen was royally fucked. To make matters worse, when she finally dared to check her phone, she had over thirty missed calls from Dolian, along with about fifty text messages that went from irritated to downright livid.

> Imogen, don't listen to her.

> She doesn't know us like I do.

> We need to talk this through.

Answer the phone, Imogen.

Is she keeping you from me?

Nothing is going to stand between us! I
won't allow it!

ANSWER YOUR PHONE IMOGEN

And so on until her very blood ran cold. For some reason, they brought to mind the reports Dylan gave her of all Dolian's supposedly violent interactions only found on the dark web. The texts were vaguely threatening, though nothing as blatant as the altercations described online, yet Imogen couldn't help but notice the underlying theme: Dolian had a dark side. And it had the potential to be very dangerous.

To make matters worse, when Imogen and Austin finally made it home, Sylvia was there and in an equally foul mood.

"My replacement was three hours late downstairs, so I missed my shift at the diner!" her mother shouted. She was in the kitchen, unnecessarily slamming pots around as she cooked dollar store macaroni and cheese. "Can you believe that? One more attendance issue like that and Vicki is gonna fire me!"

The cash Sylvia made in tips was the household's main supplement for groceries when their food stamps inevitably ran out. Losing her job at the diner would make the difference between eating and starving for their family.

"Here, Mom, let me." Imogen placed a gentle hand on her mother's elbow so that she could take her place at the stove.

Sylvia sank down into one of the kitchen chairs and stared

off into space as she mulled over her anger. Austin went to the couch to play with the small Grecian computer puzzle that the detective bought him at the farmer's market.

"What's that he's got?" Sylvia nodded towards Austin.

"Oh, just something we found," Imogen replied airily. "Can't you talk to Vicki and explain the situation?"

Her attempt to divert Sylvia's attention succeeded. Rather than pressing the issue of Austin's new trinket, she lost herself in a rant about how unfairly her boss at the diner treated everybody and how lucky Vicki was to have an employee like Sylvia in the first place. Imogen added consoling noises at the appropriate pauses while cooking.

Once plates were served to Sylvia and Austin, now happily watching a cartoon on tv, Imogen offered, "I'm sorry, Mom."

Sylvia snorted. "It's Vicki who should be sorry!"

"No, I mean I'm sorry…for earlier." She held her breath, waiting for more of Sylvia's outrage.

Instead, her mom leaned forward with a sigh. "Me, too, Im. I just want what's best for you. I'm afraid of you getting hurt. This weird obsession you've had over that guy always just seemed like a quirk. But I guess it's more than that. I don't know—I never liked something as much as you like this movie star."

Imogen smiled. "You have your own weirdness."

"That I do!" Sylvia chuckled before scooping some of the pasta into her mouth. "This is good. Thanks."

She hadn't even bothered to make herself a plate, knowing she couldn't eat with her stomach in such painful knots. "Is it okay if I run over to Dylan's real quick? He printed something off for me."

Her mother nodded. "Yeah, I guess I'll be here all night. The home is fully staffed tonight, so they don't have any hours for me to pick up."

Before her mom could change her mind, Imogen stood up and grabbed her purse. "That's good, Mom. Maybe you can finally get some sleep tonight. I promise, I'll be right back."

The buzz in her pocket let Imogen know that another text had arrived, probably from Dolian. Just in case he resorted to tracking her again, she placed the phone on the small side table by the couch before heading out the door.

When she arrived at Dylan's apartment, there were several bags of trash piled up outside. For anyone else, the sight wouldn't raise alarms, but with Dylan, taking out the garbage was highly unusual. She pounded her fist on the front door in fear.

"What the fuck, Imogen!" Dylan's sweaty face popped out as he opened the door just enough to peer out. "Are you trying to break down the door?!"

She rolled her eyes. "Of course not! But there's garbage outside!"

Dylan glanced at the bags in question. "Yeah. So?"

"So I thought that meant something bad happened!" Imogen couldn't recall a single time she'd ever seen Dylan put trash where it belonged, including back in high school where he tended to just leave things on the floor outside his locker so that the janitors would pick it up.

Dylan's face appeared redder than usual, and he wasn't opening the door to allow her inside. While Dylan always acted a little off center, this was weird, even for him.

"Why are you here?" he demanded angrily.

"Because I need you to look into something for me," Imogen began. "See, there's this guy I—"

"I don't care!" Dylan snapped, cutting her off with a glare. "I can't help you anymore, Imogen!"

He had never turned her down before. His words were laced with a bite she didn't know Dylan possessed.

"Dyl, what's going on? Why are you so flushed? What is all of this?" Imogen looked closer at one of the garbage bags and recognized the corner of a monitor Dylan used for his wall mounted space. "Are you getting rid of—"

"Bye, Imogen!" he huffed before slamming the door in her face.

"DYLAN!" Her fist beat on the door so hard that one of Dylan's neighbors opened their door to tell Imogen to shut up. A blush burned its way up her face as she mumbled an apology.

Erratic behavior wasn't exactly new for Dylan, who had always been a bit of an oddball. The gamer stereotype, if you will. But this was out in left field. Imogen didn't know what to think.

As she walked home, Imogen kept trying to remember exactly what Dylan's monitor set up looked like. There were always so many in his apartment, whether they were due to be repaired, available for scrap parts, or actively in use with his elaborate wall. But for some reason, the one in the garbage bag looked distinctive to her. Was it the brand logo on the corner?

And what could possibly be enough motivation for someone like Dylan, who never threw anything away, to chuck computer equipment he used? A replacement would have simply been put up while the old one moved to one of the piles in the room.

Thoughts swirled in Imogen's head, each one leading to a dead end, so she didn't notice when she arrived at the apartment and the front door was already open. Neither Austin, nor Sylvia were in the living room, which was for the best because Imogen wasn't ready to answer any of her mother's questions.

Imogen burst into her bedroom and pulled out her old laptop. Davani said she needed to investigate everything on the Contact herself, but her gut told her she needed to investigate Dolian, too. If the Contact made good on his threat, it could put Dolian in danger just as much as her, and Imogen didn't want to face the guilt of her worlds converging like that.

In her haste to get the computer up and running, Imogen knocked the frayed computer bag off the nightstand. When she bent down to pick it up, the press badge from the *Agent Reckless* premiere fell out. It was the first time she had really looked at it. Only now did she notice her name was nowhere to be found. There was a small photo of her face, similar to that of a driver's license, that she had to submit to security, but underneath it merely stated PRESS MEMBER.

Why did that set off a warning bell in her head?

As Imogen recalled the events of that fateful day, her encounter with Dolian stuck out clearly.

"My name?" she whispered. "How did you know my name?"

Dolian's smile dropped for barely a moment before he explained, "It's on your press badge, of course."

Except her name wasn't on her press badge. And Dolian

distinctly identified her as Ms. Reilly when he barked orders at the security guard. Imogen was certain of it.

Scrambling to her computer, Imogen logged into her email and searched for the email notifying her of the contest for the premiere. It came from the address "contest@agentrecklesspremiere.com". But when she popped "agentrecklesspremiere.com" into the internet browser, nothing came up except an offer to buy that domain name. The website didn't exist.

Scuffling sounds came from the living room, signaling that her mom and Austin must be back out. Imogen needed to maintain her composure in front of them. Sylvia would hit the roof if she learned about the Contact and the threats he sent her way.

But when Imogen entered the living room, Dolian's malicious eyes gleamed back at her.

TWENTY-FIVE

"You have to be careful with an actor as talented as Dolian…he could easily get lost in the character. A good director is gonna make sure he pulls himself back out."
-Calvin Laurent, screenwriter and film director

"Dolian!" Imogen gasped. "What are you doing here?"

The malevolent glint was back in his eyes, though he wore a tight smile. It was strained, leaving his dimples hidden. He still wore a navy peacoat over his clothes and stood in the middle of the tiny living room. Just his presence made the area seem smaller.

Austin sat on the coffee table, his eyes wide and melancholy. Imogen would have guessed that he had recently cried, though his cheeks were dry and there was no sign of a tissue. People with Down Syndrome often had runny noses since their nasal passages didn't fully develop, but his nose appeared clear.

She didn't dare take too long to examine his face,

however, because there was something about Dolian's demeanor that didn't sit well with her. One hand possessively gripped Austin's shoulder to keep her brother in place.

"Where is my mother?" Imogen asked instead. There were dozens of questions dancing in her head, but she chose what seemed like the safest.

Dolian's smile widened in a way that looked far more menacing than offered any reassurance. "Sylvia won't be bothering us again."

Confused, Imogen's brow furrowed. It was then that she noticed her Dolian Crawford binder on the coffee table beside Austin. Nobody was ever permitted to touch it, which was why she always kept it hidden underneath her bed. Imogen was positive she put it away last night when she looked at it. That was part of her nightly ritual; she wouldn't have been able to sleep without putting it back in the right place.

Her throat felt tight as she whispered, "Why do you have my book?"

Dolian grinned. "Oh, the book will be going with us. I'm quite fond of it."

Imogen blanched. Her obsession with Dolian Crawford was never meant to be public knowledge. She certainly never intended to share any of it with him. He probably thought Imogen was a freak.

"Bring it with us?" she repeated. "Bring it with us where? What do you mean?" Imogen's bottom lip started quivering as panic set in.

Dolian stepped forward, cupping both of his hands around her upper arms. "Shh," he consoled her. "Everything's going to be better now, you'll see."

She shook her head and tried to take a step back, but he firmly held her in place. "Dolian, you're hurting me," pleaded Imogen.

"Never," he breathed as he leaned down to kiss her. She was too confused to stop him, and her heart nearly beat through her chest. But Imogen could no longer tell if it was love, excitement, or absolute terror.

"Dolian," she said again, "where is my mom?"

He scowled, contorting his features into the villainous form Imogen dreaded. "Bag her," Dolian ordered to someone behind her.

But before she could turn her head, a solid black cloth wrapped around her face, and something hard and heavy struck the back of her head. The world went black.

TWENTY-SIX

"I would swoon if I ever had to do a love scene with you, Dolian. Seriously, all your co-stars must need to go home and take a cold shower after a day of filming with you!"
-Shannon Albrooks, TV host

Imogen had no concept of time or location when she woke up. Her head hurt like hell, and a tender examination with her fingers confirmed that at one point the wound bled. Now, her hair felt matted and sticky from where the blood dried. She was in a dark room by herself, lying down on what felt like a wooden bench. A sliver of light across the room indicated where the door was located. Soft voices could be heard on the other side.

Gingerly, Imogen sat up, holding one hand to her head. The pain was more of a dull throb, but she could definitely feel the knot forming on her scalp. Nothing else hurt. Once she was certain she wouldn't pass out or get dizzy, she rose and crossed to the door.

Huxley stood on the other side with his back to the door. He turned in surprise when she opened it.

"Darling!" Dolian called. His beaming face could be seen down a hall to the left, which was far brighter. Huxley turned and waved Imogen towards his employer.

She was back at The Majestic, Imogen realized. Whatever room she came from was on the opposite side of the penthouse from where she got ready for the gala. Pitch black sky outlined the city of Los Angeles from the window, meaning only a few hours had passed. Dolian had changed into dark jeans and a black utility shirt that would have normally made Imogen's mouth water. Despite the late hour, he looked wide awake and happy.

"Here, come sit down!" Dolian grabbed one of her hands and led her over to the couch, sitting beside her.

Imogen shook her head, then immediately regretted the action because of how much it hurt her head. "How did we get back here? Where's Austin? You had somebody hit me!" She made to get up, glaring accusingly at Huxley, who continued to stand stoically in the doorway to the hall from which she had just emerged.

Dolian shook his head and gave her a small smile. "Honey, you fell and hit your head. Clearly you are confused. Nobody hit you!"

Imogen blinked several times and discreetly pinched her own thigh. Was she dreaming?

"We came here after the gala," Dolian explained gently. "You were so upset after we learned what happened to Sully, and when you tried to take a shower to calm yourself, you slipped and fell. The doctor's only just left. Right, Huxley?"

She turned and looked at him for confirmation, now doubting all sense of sanity. "But the gala was yesterday…"

Her boyfriend looked at her sheepishly. "I know. And I'm sorry that you've been out of it for so long. I didn't want to add more media speculation to your plate by taking you to the hospital. I have a doctor that I keep on staff for things like this. Had he felt you needed further medical treatment, I swear we would've taken you straight away." With all the loving caress of a Regency dandy, Dolian brushed the hair from her eyes and cupped one hand around her cheek.

If Imogen had any food in her stomach, she was positive the contents would've made a reappearance. Why did she think she spent the afternoon at the farmer's market with Detective Davani?

"Where is Austin?" Imogen finally asked. "Is he okay?"

"He's fine!" assured Dolian. Wrapping an arm around her, he pulled her body close to his, tucking her head under his chin. "We are just waiting for the new caregiver to get here so that we can leave."

"Leave? What?!" Imogen bolted upright, making her vision swim before her eyes. She slumped back down to the couch and cradled her head.

Dolian beamed at her. It was the smile she loved, where his dimples popped out and his whole face lit up. The face of a movie star.

"As much as I adore your brother, sweetheart, he can't go on the honeymoon with us."

Imogen reeled backward like she had been slapped. "Honeymoon?! But we're not…!" Only as she said it did she realize that the ring finger on her left hand felt heavy as it sported a new adornment. An enormous emerald square diamond, larger than her thumbnail, rested in a platinum band surrounded by pink diamonds.

It was ostentatious, not something she would have chosen for herself, but now she was really baffled. When had they gotten engaged and why didn't she remember it?

"Dolian, you never proposed to me." Imogen's voice sounded much more confident than she felt. Broken memories of the past few days filtered through her mind, but they were like sand trickling in through a sieve.

He stiffened, the smile sliding from his face in an instant. "Yes, I did. Don't you remember?"

Imogen shook her head. Tears leaked out from the corners of her eyes. There was no way she would forget a proposal from *the* Dolian Crawford. That would have been her wildest dream coming true, even if she couldn't reconcile both sides of his personality.

Dolian nodded to Huxley, who turned and left the room. In a moment he was back with a newspaper that he handed to Imogen. The front page headline declared,

DOLIAN CRAWFORD OFFICIALLY OFF THE MARKET!

Underneath was a photograph of Imogen and Dolian at the foundation gala, where she held up a hand with the diamond ring on display. Perusing the article, it described a heartfelt speech and lavish proposal on stage in front of all the event attendees. The image looked completely foreign to Imogen, leaving her mind blank.

Imogen frowned. She didn't remember any of that happening. And how could it? She spent the end of the gala at LAPD headquarters after being arrested by Detective Davani.

"But...but this didn't happen," argued Imogen feebly. The proof was right in her hand and on her finger, so how could she doubt it? "Besides, Dolian, we've only known each other for a couple weeks!"

For once, she found his smile grating. "We're old souls, Imogen. We've known each other across lifetimes." He placed a tender kiss on her temple, his thumb rubbing along the band of her engagement ring. "This is what I've always wanted, so why wait?"

A knock on the door prevented Imogen from raising any further argument. Huxley opened the door to a social worker from the day center that Imogen recognized, but didn't know by name. The woman wore a plain green t-shirt and gray joggers, and looked as if she was trying hard to stay awake. While she might have the credentials to take care of someone like Austin, Imogen wasn't sold on the idea of leaving him with a stranger. There was nothing familiar about her that would permit Imogen's anxiety to lessen.

"Ah, thank you, Grace!" Dolian offered her a hand and the woman flushed a bright crimson. "I appreciate you coming on such short notice!"

"You're Dolian Crawford!" the woman gushed, clearly falling under his charming spell.

"I hope so or else I stole someone's wallet!" Dolian smiled warmly at her, and Grace simpered. She shook his hand like it was a precious jewel. "Please, come this way so you can get reacquainted with Austin."

He led her towards the primary bedroom, where they got

ready for the gala. She found it hard to believe it was only yesterday. It should have been lifetimes.

Imogen held up her hand to examine the heavy diamond sparkling on her finger. Not a single memory of his proposal came to mind. She vaguely remembered waking up to her mother's anger. There were newspaper headlines involved in that fight, too.

And then that horrible conversation with the Contact. Had that been a dream? A side effect from hitting her head?

"Huxley, where's my phone?" Imogen asked.

The man leveled her with a gaze, but did not reply.

Frustrated, Imogen scrambled off the couch to find Dolian and check on her brother. "Dolian, do you have my ph—my phone..." Her voice trailed off as she entered the bedroom where Austin slept. The tv was on, the credits of whatever movie he'd been watching still rolling.

But clutched in his hand was the Grecian computer puzzle that Imogen knew Detective Davani purchased for him at the farmer's market.

TWENTY-SEVEN

"We will never see another actor like Dolian Crawford in our lifetime. Now, whether or not that's a good thing, I can't say."
-Howard Badgely, Toronto film critic

Imogen tried to keep her face impassive. Given Dolian's explosive temper, she didn't want to instigate anything around Austin. In fact, she needed to do whatever she could to get Dolian as far away from Austin as possible. Everything she remembered about that day was true, including the threat the Contact made, meeting Davani at the farmer's market, and Dylan's strange behavior when she tried to garner his help. How they wound up with an engagement photo in the newspaper was still a mystery.

That meant the injury on the back of her head was by Dolian's design. She hadn't fallen and done this to herself. And there hadn't been any medical attention. Someone, Imogen assumed Huxley, struck her after Dolian ordered them to "bag" her.

They were no longer safe. Imogen wanted to get Austin home, but that would only raise further suspicions. Dolian couldn't know that she remembered the truth. Besides, Sylvia had been missing from their apartment when she got back from visiting Dylan, and Imogen couldn't help but believe Dolian and Huxley had a hand in that.

Imogen went over to her brother's sleeping form and softly kissed his head. Austin suffered from alopecia, as many people with Down Syndrome did, whereby he often lost clumps of hair. Her heart clenched as she noted another tiny spot behind his right ear lobe. Would she ever get the chance to discuss it with his doctor? In a strange way, this almost felt like goodbye.

"Imogen?" Dolian whispered. He stood in the bathroom doorway, Grace hovering just behind him.

Imogen swallowed down her tears and joined them. "I just wanted to say good night," she explained. "What are you guys doing?"

Dolian considered her response for a moment before replying. "I was just explaining Austin's bathroom needs to Grace. The nurse won't arrive for a few more hours. You have nothing to worry about, honey."

Imogen offered Grace a small smile while internally frowning. Dolian couldn't know Austin's bathroom schedule because he barely knew her brother. It was a relationship in passing. "Thank you so much for taking care of my brother. I'm relying on you to make sure he's okay. He deserves the best care."

If she found the request dramatic, Grace didn't let on. Dolian, however, frowned at her. "Grace came highly recommended. The day center said she's Austin's caseworker and one of their best employees."

Grace glowed under his praise while Imogen struggled not to roll her eyes. Caseworkers switched assignments more often than they did anything else. In all likelihood, she had never had a single conversation or interaction with Austin. The fact that Imogen barely recognized her proved that much.

Imogen offered another tight smile. "Of course, sweetheart. I trust you to take care of us."

It was the perfect thing to say. Dolian's entire face brightened and he stood taller, his chest practically puffed out with pride. Wrapping an arm around Imogen's waist, Dolian winked at the social worker. "I'm a pretty lucky guy, right?"

The woman had stars in her eyes. "I just love your love story! You don't need to worry, Mrs. Crawford. I'll take excellent care of your brother. Enjoy your honeymoon!"

Imogen paled at being addressed as such. Dolian steered them out of the room and back into the living room where Huxley waited with a couple suitcases.

"I took the liberty of having your new stylist pick everything out," Dolian informed her with a grin. "Why waste a day shopping?"

But Imogen wasn't really listening. "Dolian, why did she call me 'Mrs. Crawford'? We're not married yet."

He laughed. "It's too exciting for me to hear, so I instructed everyone to call you that from now on. Besides, in just a few short hours, that'll be your real name anyway."

The ringing in her ears might have been all in her head, but that didn't make it any less painful. "We're getting married *today*?"

"How else could we leave for a honeymoon? Wow, that fall really did a number on your head!" Dolian nodded to Huxley, who immediately started carrying the luggage out. "Don't worry, I paid a crew to transform the garden at my house into the perfect wedding oasis. It's everything you had in your book." He winked before handing over her purse.

Her book? If he was referring to her Dolian Crawford binder, that only contained news articles and photographs. There was nothing in there about a wedding, real or imaginary. She would never put a pen to paper with those thoughts as a teen—her mom already thought she was crazy. Visualizing a wedding to a mega star wasn't exactly going to prove her sanity.

"Come on," Dolian said, holding out his arm for her. "Our future awaits."

———

Four hours later, Imogen found herself in an off-white satin gown, complete with mermaid tail train. A new team of stylists, who did not speak other than to say, "Yes, Mrs. Crawford," made her look like a starlet from the Hollywood days of yore. Her soft brown hair was coiffed into curls reminiscent of Betty Grable.

And yet her hands couldn't stop shaking.

As soon as they arrived back at Dolian's remote mountain home, Imogen scoured through her things to find her cell phone. When she located it in the very bottom of the suitcase, everything was wiped clean. She no longer had any contacts other than Dolian and Huxley—not even her mother. There were no texts or pictures. All traces of her connection to the Contact were gone.

Even though she knew it was a death wish, she sent one last plea for help to the Contact, whose number she memorized. The message didn't send. "Just like Dolian told me," Imogen sighed. She recalled that fateful day when they had their interview and he gave her a house tour, he told her that the only room in the house that had any kind of reception or Wi-Fi was the security center attached to Huxley's living quarters.

Imogen wanted to curl into a ball and cry. A doe-eyed, teenage Imogen would have given anything for a day like this. Marrying Dolian Crawford, the object of her passionate obsession, was the ultimate goal. But adult Imogen didn't want to marry a man who hurt her. Who didn't include her brother on their wedding day. Sylvia was also noticeably absent and Imogen had no way to call her. Even with how much her mother despised Dolian, there was no way she would miss her only daughter's wedding. The likely answer was that she hadn't even been invited. But then again, her mother was missing when Imogen got home. Her gut told her that wasn't an accident.

She only hoped that her brother was safe. Dolian promised that Austin would stay at The Majestic until they returned and bought Austin a small townhome of his own. According to Dolian, Grace reviewed Austin's file extensively and believed he was ready to live independently.

Since Imogen still had to microwave dinosaur nuggets for him, she sincerely doubted it.

Now she was merely waiting for the sun to set so that the ceremony could start. None of the staff seemed to heed her request to speak to Dolian and when she tried to leave the guest room to go find him, Huxley had stopped her at the top of the stairs.

"Just stay there and let the professionals take care of everything," he'd told her disdainfully. His leer confirmed what she already suspected; Huxley didn't like her.

Imogen kept to her room after that. She continued to stare at the newspaper article about her engagement, finding more problematic issues with the photo the longer she stared. Her arm and hand didn't look natural as she gazed at the photograph with her new ring on display. It was almost like the photo had been doctored.

Now that the shadows grew longer from her window, the ceremony was fast approaching. Dolian insisted she wanted the wedding to be at sunset so that golden haze of light would shine as they made their vows. Supposedly it was all in her book, or so he said on the drive up. Imogen didn't even know who was on the guest list.

One of the stylists came in to check her one more time before informing her that they were ready for her downstairs. Handing Imogen a bouquet of white orchids and calla lilies that cascaded down over her hands, the woman swept from the room. It also meant Imogen could keep her cell phone concealed since her wedding dress didn't have pockets. A gut instinct told her to keep her phone on her at all costs. The Contact might be the only one who could save her now, if she could get a message to him…assuming he didn't kill her first.

"You just need to keep Austin safe. You can find a way out of this," Imogen muttered to herself. Now if only her legs didn't feel like jelly.

She was surprised to see only a handful of people assembled on the balcony, where the ceremony was to take place. A reception in the garden maze would follow. Dolian met her at the bottom of the spiral staircase. He looked radiant in a black tuxedo and his hair artfully tousled so that it fell into his eyes, and if Imogen didn't know any better, she would've guessed that he wore a little make up, too. There were tears welling in the corners of his eyes, tears that he laughed at as he swiped them away before taking her hand.

"Imogen…my god, I'm the luckiest man in the world. You look spectacular," Dolian breathed. Raising one of her hands, he kissed the top, and despite her anxiety, Imogen blushed. So much of her yearned to believe it was true, that it was possible for Dolian Crawford to gaze at her with such reverent adoration. This was more than she ever dared to want as a teenager.

Dolian had been considerate enough to have a makeshift glass floor placed over the portion of the pool in the living room. Imogen didn't recognize any of the guests mingling there, which brought the stark reality of her situation crashing back. This wasn't a wedding she wanted. She was trapped and only needed to find a way out so that she could make her way back to Los Angeles and collect her brother.

That realization made her hesitate long enough to pull her hand from Dolian's grasp. Whimpering, her bottom lip began to tremble again as she shook her head. The knot on her head was still there, hiding under her veil, where he had allowed someone to hit her in his desperation to make this farce of a wedding happen. That was the kind of person he was. Not the fantasy Imogen envisioned in her dreams.

Sometimes schoolgirl crushes fade. Other times they shatter.

TWENTY-EIGHT

> *"Whoever this Imogen Reilly woman is, I hope she knows that
> millions of women want her dead!"*
> *-Marie Ellison, radio host*

Hiking up her skirts, Imogen ran around the cluster of couches and chairs to go down the stone hallway. If all of the doors were closed in the foyer, she would have no idea where to go or how to get out, but she had to try.

"IMOGEN!" Dolian bellowed after her.

Huxley's voice faintly carried after her asking all the guests to move to the balcony because there was some sort of emergency. "It will only be a moment," he promised.

Not if I can help it, Imogen thought.

The circular foyer was filled with flowers and creamy satin decorations. The fragrant smell made her nose pucker. They reminded her of funeral arrangements. Or maybe that was the fear getting to her head.

Footsteps echoed loudly behind her and without thinking,

Imogen yanked open one of the doors and dove inside, closing it as quietly as possible so there was no clue as to which she entered. It was another dark stone hallway with a faint light strip along the bottom where the floor met the wall. Dolian hadn't shown this part of his house during their tour. Supposedly it was the security office…where there was phone access!

Imogen tugged off her kitten heels so that there wouldn't be an echo on the stone as she raced down the hallway. Finding a door on the right, she pushed through and hastily closed it behind her. The cell phone clutched in her hand only showed two bars, but it was enough for the message to the Contact to send.

Clamping a hand over her mouth, Imogen looked up and had to stifle a gasp. The room looked like the kind of room Dylan would never leave. There were four tables with multiple computer monitors each. Low blue lights gave the space an eerie feel as well as illuminated the metal lockers along the back wall that held the computer servers.

Three large flat screens displayed what Imogen assumed to be a live feed of the grounds outside the house. One showed the gravel driveway and fountain where guests were getting into limousines and elite SUV's to leave. Another showed the entrance to the garden area that displayed more white flowers to match the wedding décor. The third screen showed a space outside that Imogen hadn't seen before. There was a small space where the waterfall from the infinity pool collected, but the gravel driveway looped underneath it to reveal an open underground garage of sorts. She could just make out the hood of a few cars in the darkness.

A curious buzzing sound came from one of the drawers at

the computer desk. Hoping to silence it and avoid alerting anyone to her presence, Imogen opened it to find a burner phone that buzzed with a text alert. She yelped when she glanced at the screen…and saw her plea to the Contact.

Dolian Crawford was the Contact! Imogen couldn't help it. Her stomach heaved up bile all over the stone floor.

Imogen didn't see Huxley or Dolian on any of the screens, meaning one or the both of them could burst through the door at any minute. She quickly rounded one of the desks and typed in the website for the LAPD. Typing in DAVANI in the internal search bar brought up his contact information. Imogen hoped that he checked his messages regularly as she fired off a quick alert to his email, telling him where she was and that she needed his help because she was in danger. She couldn't provide him with the exact address, but he could try to locate the IP address. That was now her only hope.

Just as her finger hit ENTER to send it, Huxley threw open the door. She cried out, ducking under the table and tried to crawl away, only for him to grab her by the ankles and drag her back. The uneven stone floor scraped at her arms and face, snagging against the silk of her dress. Bucking, Imogen tried, unsuccessfully, to flip over onto her back so she had enough leverage to kick Huxley off.

He descended on her, straddling her legs and pinning her arms over her head with a bitter snarl. "Stop fighting, Imogen! You're the one he chose! STOP!"

Fear paralyzed her to the point that she froze underneath him. What did he mean that Dolian *chose* her? Chose her for what? Over whom?

"In here! IN HERE!" Huxley bellowed. Dolian shoved

past him, yanking Imogen up by her hair. He looked murderous, his face scarlet with rage.

"Come along, *wife!*" he exploded.

Imogen screamed. She could feel the hair pulling from her scalp where she already had a recovering wound. Her skin burned in protest, and she kicked out without any traction. Although she had stockings on her feet, they weren't enough to create friction on the stone.

Dolian dragged her all the way out to the living room, where a man stood in a three piece brown suit. The man looked aghast to see her in such a state.

"Mi—mister Crawford!" he sputtered. His glasses went askew on his nose as he jumped up from the chair.

"Did you sign all the paperwork, Reverend? Are we married?" Dolian demanded.

"Y-yes, s-sir!" The reverend held up both of his hands in surrender. "Just as soon as she signs it!"

"Oh, she will." With that, Dolian pulled a pistol out of the back waistband of his pants and shot the man in the chest. Imogen couldn't hear the man's body fall over her screams.

"See, darling?" He reeled back, yanking Imogen upward so she was on her feet. "Now I get to kiss my bride!" There was no love or kindness in the kiss he seared to her lips.

Sobs racked her body. Imogen didn't even try to push him off. She couldn't accept the version of Dolian who stood before her."Why are you doing this?" she cried.

As soon as he released his arm from her waist, Imogen dropped to the floor. She immediately began crawling backward to put some distance between them.

"Because I love you, of course!" Dolian's maniacal smile

returned, the one that made him look like a deranged villain. Imogen didn't know which version of Dolian was the real one. Quite frankly, Dolian probably didn't either.

Huxley returned, standing in front of the hallway.

"Ah, Huxley! Just in time! May I introduce you to Imogen Crawford, my beautiful wife."

To her surprise, Huxley's face soured. "So you went through with it? You married her?"

Dolian's responding sigh was heavy, full of a weariness that implied he was sick of having the same conversation. "Huxley...do not start with this."

"No, why don't you go ahead and tell her the truth!" Huxley snapped. "Let her know the *real* Dolian Crawford!" He charged forward so that they were standing chest to chest.

His statement triggered Dolian in a way that Imogen didn't expect. A tick twitched in one of Dolian's eyes like he fought an apoplectic fit. They held each other's gazes in a standoff, neither willing to back down.

Huxley's chest heaved. "Tell her, Dolian! Tell her or I will!"

As quietly as possible, Imogen started to scoot back to the hallway. Neither of them bound her hands or feet. She needed to *leave*.

Dolian zeroed in on her exit. "Oh no, my love, you're not going anywhere!" In two strides, he was at her side and hauling her up around the middle to deposit on a loveseat. "Since my esteemed colleague over here wants you to know the truth, it's time that we have that discussion!"

Imogen pushed herself upright. This Dolian terrified her. The malicious gleam was becoming a permanent facial feature. He paced before her like a man unhinged, and Imogen had no idea if he even knew what reality he currently resided in. This wasn't a man who had a firm grip on his circumstances.

"Peabody Community College!" Dolian suddenly spit out. Running his fingers through his hair, he sat on the coffee table across from her, bracing his elbows on his knees. "D'you remember it?"

"Wh-what?" Imogen gasped.

"The very first entertainment article you ever wrote," he prompted. "Peabody Community College."

Imogen bounced in her seat. The school bus was bumpy as it traveled through the rough streets of Whittier, California. Her journalism class was on the way to see a play at a local college and it was her first chance to write an entertainment article for their school newspaper. She was giddy with excitement. Journalism was the only class she excelled in. Mrs. Ferguson promised to give her a weekly column if she did a good job on the play review.

It was a production of The Death of a Salesman, *an American classic that they studied in Imogen's regular English class in preparation for the field trip. Imogen had a list of notes about the history, production, and famous renditions of the play. She wanted so badly to be good at something—to prove that she could do something worthwhile. Maybe if her mother saw Imogen's column in the newspaper, it would make her notice Imogen for once. It wasn't her brother's fault that he needed so much more attention, but she couldn't help but resent it a little. There was so much to do for Austin that there was rarely any time left for her.*

All of that would change if she wrote a great article today.

Once the play ended, the class would get to go backstage and meet the cast, director, and production crew. Imogen was especially excited about that part; it was almost like being a part of Hollywood. Maybe one of the people they met would grow up to be famous!

"The play," breathed Imogen. Her lungs couldn't fill with air, no matter how hard she tried. *"Death of a Salesman."*

Dolian gave her an evil grin. "Yes. Go on."

The play was a bit of a dud, if Imogen were being completely honest. Most of the actors only seemed to participate for extra credit in one of their classes. Only one of them stood out to Imogen. The boy who played the part of Biff. Imogen estimated him to be a freshman or sophomore, with gangly limbs and a thin face. While he might not be the best looking guy out there, he was the only person on stage with enough talent to make his character believable. She couldn't take her eyes off him; his performance was mesmerizing.

As the students gathered backstage, breaking off into pairs and trios with some of the people from Peabody, Imogen only looked for the guy who played Biff. He was one of the last people to emerge, dark hair damp as though he rushed through a shower. Imogen watched as he made a beeline for the snack table, stuffing as many of the complimentary cookies into his mouth as would fit, before tucking himself into a corner.

"You were amazing!" babbled Imogen. Because of her responsibilities at home, she didn't have many friends. Most of the kids at her school thought she was weird. This was the first conversation she could ever remember initiating...and with an older boy, no less!

Crumbs fell out of his mouth as he tried to thank her. They both diverted their eyes in embarrassment. The boy swallowed and wiped his hand on his jeans. "Uh, thanks. I'm Malcolm. Malcolm Crezienski."

Imogen shook her head to bring her mind to the present moment. "Malcolm," she whispered. "You're Malcolm Crezienski."

The laugh that gurgled from Dolian's mouth sounded inhuman. This wasn't the actor she had idolized for nearly a decade. This was all Malcolm, the odd boy who dazzled on stage during a school play. How had she missed it before?

"The way you fawned over me!" Dolian continued. "You hung on me for hours, giving me every compliment you could think of, promising me that you were going to write the best review of the play. You were just adorable, Imogen!

"But then the article you sent…now, that was spectacular! So much praise for such a small production. You made me see that I not only *could* be the greatest actor the world has ever known, but that I *should* be. Dolian Crawford is because of you." He accentuated the last three words slowly, worshipfully, once again gazing at her as though the very sun rose and set because of Imogen.

She was going to be sick.

"I would do whatever it took to earn your praise again. To be worthy of the actor you saw me as. It took some plastic surgery, I'll admit, and a bit of a ruthlessness I don't quite enjoy, but now that it's led me back to you…now that we can be together forever…I've waited so long for the chance to see you again." A hand tenderly brushed across her cheek. "Now that I have you, I will be unstoppable!"

"But that's not why you marry someone!" Imogen cried, jerking away from his hand in disgust.

Dolian threw his head back and laughed, the same maniacal roar as before. Standing up, he threw out his arms and turned as if there were others watching who would agree with him. "You mean for the same reasons you wanted to marry me?! Everything I have done has always been for you, Imogen! You wanted me to be the best, so I became the best.

It was always about getting your attention because you're my muse! You are the one who helps me shine!"

Leaning down so that his nose was nearly touching hers, Imogen's blood turned to ice as he growled, "Don't you see, dear? I'm your number one fan!"

TWENTY-NINE

*"Chameleons have a harder time changing colors than Dolian
Crawford. Truly, the man's a genius!"*
-Devin Holiwell, movie producer

The gun shot that rang out startled both Imogen and Dolian. She ducked as stone debris fell down from the ceiling where the bullet landed. Huxley stood with his hand raised over his head, gun pointed upward. Imogen noted that his finger remained on the trigger. A finger that was visibly shaking with rage as he glared at Dolian.

"You weren't supposed to love her, Dolian! That wasn't our deal!"

Dolian approached Huxley slowly, both hands raised as a peace offering. The gun Huxley now pointed at his employer's chest was the same gun Dolian used to kill the reverend. Imogen wondered who it actually belonged to because Huxley looked ready to fire directly into Dolian's heart.

"Huxley...we've talked about this," Dolian said consolingly, his voice as smooth as silk. "I don't feel that way about you. I'm sorry!"

Huxley pointed the gun upward again, firing into the stone ceiling. Imogen screamed as more debris fell down around her, the gunshot echoing in the cavernous space. She clamped her hands over her ears and dove to the wall, crouching down to protect herself.

"I *killed* for you!" Huxley's face turned an ugly shade of crimson. The vein in his forehead throbbed as if threatening to burst. "I cleaned up every mess you made! You told me you needed her to make you the biggest star in the world! Not because you *loved* her!"

"You're the Contact," Imogen whimpered as the realization hit. Something about the disgust in his voice triggered the idea. Slowly, she stood, pinning her back against the wall. "That's why you always tried to talk me out of pursuing things with Dolian."

Huxley's black eyes burned through her. "You don't deserve him! *I'm* Dolian's biggest fan! I walked out on my marriage—on my kid—for YOU!" He shoved Dolian so hard in the chest that the actor fell backward and landed hard on his head. A groan came from his mouth on impact before he stilled.

Imogen's eyes streamed with tears. She made no move to stop them, too paralyzed with fear. "Did you kill Jesse Ramirez and Evette Coleman? Did you kill *Sully?*" she whispered in horror.

Rather than answer, Huxley rolled his eyes. "And my son thinks you're so smart. You're an idiot, Imogen! Everything I've told you as the Contact has always been true! No one will care when I wipe you off this planet." The gun swung back in her direction. "I didn't kill that guard. Dolian became irate over how that security guard treated you and strangled him in a rage. I knew something like that would ruin him, so I killed Evette as a way to take the heat off him."

"And put it right back on me," Imogen added. "You knew everyone saw our altercation that night. The police had every reason to believe I did it."

Huxley smirked at her. "That was an added bonus. Your precious Sully dared to confront Dolian over the way he treated you. As if Dolian could be anything other than perfect. Sully had to go after that."

Imogen's limbs went numb. It was sickening to hear Huxley's hero-worship of Dolian. If that was how she sounded all these years, it was no wonder her mother hated the actor.

"And my mother?" she asked. "Where is she? Did you do something to her?"

The scars on his face looked menacing in the pale light. Huxley could have been the reaper, a figment from her worst nightmares sent to ruin her life. "Your mother had to pay for the way she talked to Dolian."

"What did you do?" Imogen's eyes drifted down to Dolian, but right then, Dylan walked into the room. He glared at Huxley without so much as a second glance at Imogen.

"I did what you asked," Dylan told him. "All the major news stations will get the statement first thing in the morning. Should be enough time to be the morning headline."

"Good, good," Huxley mumbled. His eyes stayed trained on Imogen. The hand continued to shake with his finger on the trigger. "It's about time! What took you so long?"

Imogen could have been knocked over just from the finger alone. How did Dylan know Huxley?

She vaguely remembered a time in high school where Dylan struggled because his dad walked out on their family, but they were never close enough as friends for Imogen to know the real story. Try as hard as she might, his father's name escaped her. Could it be Huxley? Had he left them for Dolian?

"Dylan…" Her voice quivered as she tried to control the sobs that wanted to come out. "Did you help him do this to me?"

Hard eyes turned towards her. Now that Dylan stood next to Huxley, the resemblance was obvious. There was no reason for her to have missed it, and she cursed her carelessness. "It's nothing personal, Imogen," Dylan offered with a shrug. "You're just collateral damage. Dropping all those fake articles in your hand and blasting your pap shots to the media meant I had money to live on."

She bristled. "My face was all over the tabloids because of *you?!*"

Again, he shrugged, not a care in the world. Instead, he turned to Huxley and said, "That money better be in my account by midnight."

Huxley waved him off, like someone at a picnic swatting a fly. "Yeah, you'll get your money. Stay here so you can help me with the body."

Imogen's heart began to race and her stomach clenched. Dolian finally started to rouse, rubbing his head and gingerly sitting upright. When he realized that Huxley had the gun pointed towards Imogen, he jumped to his feet, moving to stand in front of her.

"Your issue is with me, Huxley," he moaned, one hand still cradling the back of his head. "Don't take it out on her!"

His assistant's face contorted as he succumbed to sobs. "No, my issue is with her! We were happy without her! Why did you have to go and ruin everything by getting married? *I love you!*"

Even Dylan looked ready to gag. Nausea threatened to purge the bile burning in Imogen's stomach. Dolian continued to stand between her and the gun, slowly inching forward so as not to startle Huxley into pulling the trigger. It was only then that she noticed the hand on the back of Dolian's head was frantically pointing towards the doorway. He wanted her to run.

But Dylan stood before it, and with Imogen's tiny size, she doubted she could move him to make it out. Still, she had to try.

When Dolian moved close enough to Huxley that he finally lowered the weapon, blubbering about how much he loved Dolian and how he would do anything for him, Dylan angrily winced. He spun on his heel, tearing off down the hall, eager to escape the emotional display.

Imogen only hesitated for a moment before racing after him. As soon as she reached the shadows of the hall, Huxley let out a roar like a wounded bear.

"YOU TRICKED ME!"

Sounds of a scuffle followed before the gun went off again, but Imogen didn't dare check to see where the bullet landed. Dylan also heard the blast, and started back towards her. This was the worst episode of Scooby-Doo Imogen had ever seen, with the fat lump of a man stalking her way, arms outstretched to trap her.

Going back wasn't an option. "You don't need to do this, Dylan!" she pleaded. "We're friends!"

"You were never my friend!" scoffed Dylan. "I only helped you so that I could keep tabs on you for my dad! That was the only way he would love me!"

Despite her predicament, Imogen's heart broke for him. She knew exactly what that felt like. But she would never sacrifice another person to get Sylvia's love. "I'm sorry, Dylan." Imogen really did feel bad for him, and guilty for what she was about to do.

Throwing all of her strength into it, Imogen bent at the waist and barreled towards him as fast as she could. Surprise registered on Dylan's face as the momentum carried her forward, crashing into his abdomen with enough force to knock the wind out of him. Clambering off his stomach, Imogen stomped on his groin with all her might. Dylan howled like a wolf in pain.

Another gunshot spurred her forward. One of them would be on her heels in an instant, and she honestly didn't know which was the worse option. Her only chance of survival was getting out of this house. Imogen sent up a silent prayer that Detective Davani received her message.

Back out in the circular foyer, Imogen dove for a door to the right instead of left like last time. Everything was pitch black on the other side. She stepped forward without realizing it was a staircase, and tumbled, headfirst, down the entire flight. The crash landing at the bottom was loud enough to wake the dead. They definitely knew where she was.

"Oh, god!" Imogen groaned, too beaten up to care about her volume. There was a shooting pain radiating from one of her wrists and her left ankle twisted in an unnatural direction. She could already feel the bruises forming everywhere else. Standing up proved that Imogen couldn't manage weight for very long on her left foot, and she bit down hard on her lip to keep from crying out. Heavy footsteps thundered overhead.

At first glance, Imogen was in some sort of makeshift mudroom. There were racks of coats and shoes along the walls, with a closed door to her left and a closed door on the wall opposite. She chose the one across since it was closest and darted inside just as a light flicked on at the top of the staircase.

An old overhead light came on, motion activated, as Imogen shivered. The room resembled a walk in freezer, with ice coating the walls and floors. She turned away from the door to see if the space had another exit when she let out a bloodcurdling scream.

Sylvia's body, frozen solid with eyes still gaping in permanent horror, laid on a shelf before her.

The scream couldn't stop. Imogen no longer knew how. When Dylan and Huxley burst into the room behind her, she continued to shriek, like a banshee in training. It was only when Huxley cuffed her with the butt of the gun that the screams finally stopped.

THIRTY

"I have been so fortunate to have so many great opportunities come my way. But, you know, at some point, the luck's gotta run out, right?"
-Dolian Crawford, documentary

Pain so acute that Imogen wanted to die sliced through her ankle and head. Rivulets of blood trailed down the side of her face when she woke up back in the living room of Dolian's house. Her hands were tied behind her back with a scrap of her veil while a rope bound her ankles, only her bad ankle had been pushed even farther in the wrong direction. Judging by the searing pain, it was definitely broken now.

She barely managed to muffle a scream when she saw Dolian's body beside her. His breathing was shallow, skin a pasty white, and there was a gun shot wound bleeding from his left abdomen. A thin sheen of sweat lined his forehead, but his eyes were closed. If not for the subtle rise and fall of his chest, Imogen would presume him dead.

Dylan and Huxley were having a heated argument close to

the pool. They both gesticulated wildly, the gun still in Huxley's hand.

"I didn't sign on to help you murder somebody!" Dylan shouted. "How many is that gonna be now, Dad? Four? Five?"

His dad's skin was a motley array of purple as he tried to get a grip on his fury. "I didn't kill that security guard! If that moron wouldn't have killed the guy for breaking the bitch's phone, I wouldn't have had to kill Evette!"

Dylan grunted in frustration. "Oh my god, do you even *hear* yourself?! Do you know how fucked up all of this is? You're the one who came to me about that stupid fake newspaper with the doctored engagement photo! You're the one who told me to keep an eye on the security footage at The Majestic in case she showed up! This is all your fault, and I don't wanna go to prison because of you!"

"You're not gonna go to prison." Huxley sneered at his son in condescension. "Guys like you don't go to prison. Just help me kill her and get the bodies buried out in the yard, and I'll send the two million to your account."

"Five million!" Dylan pointed towards the hall. "Five million or I walk, and I'll walk straight to the police! I didn't ask to be dragged into this freak show. I want my money and a private plane to Mexico."

Standing straighter, Huxley glared at Dylan. "Then why did you send her that phony internet contest? You think I don't know it was you?! I might not be a computer genius like you, but I know enough to know that you set all this up from the beginning!"

Imogen remained frozen, too terrified to even breathe. Dylan was the one who sent her the email contest for the

Agent Reckless premiere! That was how she won—how she got to meet Dolian in the first place.

And all while Huxley acted as the Contact. Just to keep her away from Dolian.

"The madness wasn't gonna end any other way, Dad!" Dylan shot back.

The lights flashed before cutting out completely as an alarm rang loudly throughout the house before Huxley had the chance to respond.

"What's that?!" There was just enough moonlight shining through the windows for Imogen to see the outlines of their figures. Dylan had tensed, frantically whirling about to locate the source of the noise. But Huxley straightened to his full height. Scowling, he held up the gun in front of him.

"That's the alarm from the front gate. Someone's here!"

Neither of them looked in Imogen's direction as they both headed towards the foyer.

That meant Imogen didn't have a second to waste. She hoped it was Davani at the gate for her, but she had no way of knowing. Police wouldn't cut off power to someone's home during a rescue, would they? Had she ever heard about that on a true crime podcast?

As her shoulders burned in protest, Imogen hiked her knees up to her chin, folding her legs in as close to her chest as she could. Her waif-like size finally came in handy as she managed to loop her arms underneath her ass and around the front of her knees. It was enough that she bent forward to untie the rope from around her legs.

None of the bedrooms had access to a secondary exit, and there was no sense in going to the main foyer where Huxley and Dylan would be waiting. The only way out as far as she knew was to go onto the balcony.

But when she went to the window, she couldn't find the hidden spot that opened into a door. Given the odd technology of the building, Imogen wouldn't have been surprised if it only opened under Dolian's fingerprints. There was no other way out. She was trapped.

Unless...

Imogen eyed the pool with sickening dread. She would have to completely submerge herself under the water to swim under the thick plated glass to get outside. Once on the balcony, there was a stairwell that went down to the garages. If nothing else, maybe she could drive off in one of the cars in Dolian's open garage.

But could her phobia allow her entry in the pool to begin with?

"There's more of them!"

Imogen heard Dylan's distant shout only seconds before gunfire reverberated on the stone walls. She needed to get away from the fighting or else Huxley would turn that gun on her.

Going into the pool was the only way.

Silent sobs choked her as she kneeled beside the pool. Her hands shook so bad that she almost couldn't grip the edge of the plated dance floor. There wasn't time for her to remove them all, so she settled with the one on the edge of the water and braced herself as she lowered the bottom half of her body in.

A panic attack clawed its way up her throat, closing off her airway. She couldn't breathe, couldn't even see as darkness closed in around the edges of her vision. Images of

Austin face down in the water, flailing around to try and save himself clouded her mind. She was going to drown, only this time it would be for real. It was poetic really that she die the same way she almost killed someone as sweet and innocent as Austin.

Dylan ran into the room, panting hard and clutching his side, a gun now in his other hand. "Dad, she's getting away!" he yelled.

So Imogen was dead either way. Submerging herself under water, the faint *tink* from where the bullet missed sounded muffled.

All she needed was to swim a few feet at most. Just a few feet and she could get out, get to safety.

If only her limbs would cooperate. If only the panic didn't convince her that she was already dead. If only her body didn't turn into dead weight, sinking towards the bottom like a stone. Imogen wasn't going to make it. The pool was just like the pool as a child, and the chlorine burned through her nose. She wanted to breathe, needed to breathe, if she could just get a breath...

Imogen's head broke through the surface of the pool outside, air scorching her esophagus, as she gulped it into her system. Both hands braced on the stone, still tied together with fabric from her veil, so she could hoist herself out when another shot rang through the air, close enough that Imogen felt the air move as the bullet whizzed past her face. Petrified, she fell back down into the water, submerged once more, as the current carrying water to the edge of the infinity pool pushed her forward.

Suddenly, there was the edge, and Imogen only just managed to grab on. Water sprayed into her face, making it difficult to breathe and see, as she held on for dear life. The stone ledge scraped against her palms, and the wet satin clinging to her skin weighed her down. She was not an athlete and had no muscle tone to speak of, making her arms go numb with the effort to hold on.

Huxley peered over the balcony, aiming a gun at her. "You should've left Dolian alone like I told you!" he roared. "None of this would have happened if you would've listened to me!"

Dylan's face appeared, looking down at her in alarm. "Dad, I'm out of bullets! The cops are everywhere! We're surrounded!"

It was only a split second before Huxley turned his elbow upward so that the gun went off, striking Dylan in the middle of the forehead. Imogen let out an earth shattering scream. Dylan's body slumped down and out of sight.

"Why are you doing this?" she cried, tears for the friend she believed Dylan to be streaming down her face.

Huxley scowled. "You were always his obsession! Even after I gave him every last cent I had, all he ever talked about was your pathetic article. Like I wasn't the one who made him Dolian Crawford!"

Imogen sobbed. Her grip started to slip as her fingers went numb.

"And now it's your turn, Imogen!" Huxley snarled. "Nobody can love Dolian Crawford more than me!"

Imogen read somewhere before that trauma could turn experiences into slow motion reels. Facing the barrel of the gun was like that, where her options were to let go and fall to her death in the shallow stone pool below or stare at the bullet coming right for her. It wasn't the kind of moment where life flashed before her eyes. She only thought of all her favorite movies, most of them Dolian Crawford films. The scene in *Passions* where she first fell in love with his hunky form as he crashed the school pep rally. Or the scene from one of his indie flicks, *Hunt for Camelot*, where he convinced the villagers to rally around the protagonist's cause so that they would all go down fighting the good fight. His speech was so moving in that movie, and he didn't get nearly enough credit for it.

The majority of her life had been spent worshiping Dolian.

And now, Imogen was prepared to die because of him. Bracing herself, shoulders clenched and eyes squeezed tight, Imogen held her breath.

BOOM!

The gunfire exploded, deafening her eardrums, but she didn't feel any pain. Peaking one eye open, she saw Huxley's body dangling over the ledge. A round bullet hole, dead center on his forehead, oozed bright red blood.

Detective Davani's face appeared in the pool. Laying flat on his stomach so that both his arms hung over the edge, he gripped Imogen's arms tightly just below her armpits. She clenched his arms above the elbow as he hauled her up and over, back into the pool. He had a rope tied around his waist that extended back to three other officers, who each helped pull them out of the pool.

Imogen scrambled to get out of the water, curling up into the fetal position. The adrenaline crash came swiftly, and even the wild tremors her body experienced couldn't keep her from passing out.

THIRTY-ONE

"Dolian should still be remembered for the incredible actor he was. Talent is talent, and he had that in spades. We are all blessed to have caught a glimpse of it."
-Imogen Reilly-Crawford, Dolian's widow

ONE YEAR LATER

A strong breeze blew through the cemetery as Imogen placed the bouquet on her mother's grave. The black marble headstone shined under the bright sun, and she was grateful for a beautiful day to visit. It would be her last visit with Sylvia since the moving truck left earlier that morning to start the three day drive out to St. Louis, Missouri, where their new home awaited.

Saying goodbye to Sylvia was bittersweet. Imogen hated to leave her behind, but she was definitely looking forward to the new life she would start with Austin. St. Louis had a reputable hospital and resources for people with Down

Syndrome, and it was far enough removed from L.A. that she didn't worry about Dolian's legacy following them.

"We're gonna be so much better off," Imogen said, whether to reassure herself or Sylvia, she didn't know. "This is the fresh start we need."

Softly, she kissed her fingertips and placed them on the top of the headstone. Black sunglasses shielded her eyes, but they couldn't block the tear that trickled down her cheek. Her mother deserved so much more than what she got in life. Imogen had long since accepted that the guilt would never go away.

Walking down to the paved path where a golf cart awaited, Imogen nodded to Miguel, her bodyguard. He sat in the driver's seat, cart idling, so that he could take them back to the main mausoleum where Dolian's body rested. Like always, she had to coordinate with cemetery staff to close the mausoleum for the day so she could pay her respects to her husband.

It took Imogen months to come to terms with her situation. Dolian held onto life for roughly six weeks after their wedding day, never able to leave the hospital as he fought for his life. Ultimately, there was too much internal damage from where the bullet hit and his body couldn't withstand the trauma. Imogen held his hand as he took his last breath.

Nobody ever knew the truth, that Dolian was the one to murder Jesse Ramirez, the security guard, or the reverend, and Imogen let Huxley take the fall for all of it. She could never articulate why it mattered, but the thought of murder tarnishing Dolian's memory hurt too much. Once she woke up in the hospital the day after her brush with death, Imogen realized that everything Dolian did stemmed from love. Ultimately, his frantic gesture behind his head could have made the difference between life and death. He was the white knight of her dreams after all.

When the police questioned her after the incident, she told them that Huxley was an obsessed fan who lost hold on reality when Dolian announced their relationship. Things escalated too much, and people who posed threats to Dolian —in Huxley's mind—paid the price for it.

While everything about his methods was wrong, it was an obsessive love for Imogen that motivated Dolian's actions. And if Imogen couldn't empathize with that, then what *could* she empathize with? She knew all too well how much desire and attraction could consume a person. How passionate one could be about the things that mattered most to them. And in the end, whether logical or not, it was the same kind of burning feeling Imogen returned for Dolian.

It was better to live as Dolian Crawford's loving widow than to hide as Dolian Crawford's biggest fan.

Not only had they not signed a prenuptial agreement, but in preparation for their wedding, Dolian had altered his will to leave everything to Imogen. Upon his death, she inherited over $250 million between his various properties, businesses, endorsements, and other assets. Since he didn't have any other family and the only employee who could have objected was dead, the courts honored Dolian's wishes. In less than one day, Imogen became a multi-millionaire and the sole owner of all Dolian Crawford proprietary rights, which had the capacity to reach billionaire status by the end of Imogen's lifetime. Not to mention the job offers from major news outlets, the publishers who wanted exclusive rights to her tell-all memoir, and studios willing to drop a fortune to create the Dolian Crawford biopic. Imogen would never want for anything again in her life.

Sadly, what she wanted most was the chance to have a real marriage with Dolian. They would have been happy, traveling the world together while he filmed on location and she cared for Austin and his needs. Dolian would have fulfilled her every need and want, Imogen convinced herself. The Dolian of her teenage dreams would have been real.

Imogen found Detective Davani inside the mausoleum, still wearing his usual jeans and open button down shirt combo. He stood with his back to her, arms crossed, as he gazed up at the six foot high stone mosaic of her favorite Dolian photograph she'd had commissioned for the location. On normal days, it was open to the public so that fans could visit. Staff told her they had to clear out flowers and gifts that fans left behind at least five times per day.

Today, it was all hers.

"Good afternoon, Detective," she greeted, coming up to stand beside him.

He turned, giving her a lazy smile, and she realized he held a manilla folder in his hand. Noticing where her eyes went, Davani held it out to her. "Final paperwork from the judge for the murders of Evette Coleman, Jesse Ramirez, Charles Sullivan, Reverend Peter Meyers, and Sylvia Reilly. Tony Huxley was identified as the perpetrator on all counts. Wasn't sure if you wanted to take a look."

Imogen gave him a small smile in return, but shook her head. "I already experienced it. I don't need to see the judge's seal to know it's real."

He chuckled sheepishly. "Yeah, I guess so. Where's Austin?"

"Back at the house with his new companion."

Now that Imogen had the money to do so, she kept an entire live-in staff employed to help meet Austin's needs. Joey was Austin's "companion," a term she used loosely to describe someone that she merely employed to be Austin's friend. Joey had the patience of a saint, never tiring of superhero movies and coloring books, and catering to Austin's every whim. They had so much fun together, which really brought Austin out of his shell. Joey was now the one who took care of all of Austin's therapies and appointments. It gave Imogen the freedom to simply love Austin as a sister. Something she discovered was far superior to resenting him as a caregiver.

They also kept a nurse named Gillian on staff in case Austin had any medical issues. The peace of mind Imogen felt from being able to provide that level of care to Austin was worth any price tag. And it would be even better in St. Louis, where they could retain a level of anonymity Imogen could no longer achieve in the Valley.

"Well, tell him I said goodbye." Davani gestured towards her stomach, eyebrows raised in question. "Are you sure you're ready for this?"

Imogen cradled her small baby bump with both arms, practically purring with delight. Nodding tearfully, she smiled at the detective. "Yeah, I am."

On one of the rare days where Dolian was coherent enough to talk with her before his death, Imogen lamented over the fact that they might never have a baby. Surgeons had already attempted to repair Dolian's injuries twice, but his prognosis wasn't good. They were both anticipating the end.

Saving his sperm had been Dolian's idea. He made her swear to use it someday when she was ready to be a mother.

"It would be an honor to carry your child," Imogen had cooed. And because money was the magic wand that made things happen in Los Angeles, Dolian's doctors had agreed, preserving his sperm in a private bank, accessible only to Imogen. They even met with a team of fertility doctors to ensure when Imogen was ready to get pregnant, there would be nothing stopping her.

Once the plans to relocate were in place, Imogen knew it was the right time. She wanted to take a little piece of Dolian with her to Missouri. Her little peanut would arrive in roughly fourteen weeks, and Imogen couldn't wait to find out if she was having a boy or a girl.

"Then this is goodbye, I guess." The detective held out a hand, but Imogen pulled him into a hug instead.

"Thank you for everything, Davani," whispered Imogen. "I'm grateful to put this all behind me."

With a final wave, the detective left the mausoleum, leaving her alone with Dolian's remains. She placed another large bouquet of flowers at the base of the mosaic and departed.

The ride home was peaceful as Miguel drove them through West Hollywood and into Brentwood, where she had purchased a small home shortly after Dolian's passing. All of the other properties, including The Majestic, had been sold off. Imogen figured it was like ripping off a Band-aid. Better to do it all at once and be done with it than to hold onto properties piece by piece for nostalgia's sake. She forgave Dolian for what he did to make her his wife, but she was ready to leave this part of her life behind. Thanks to the comfortable living his movies would continue to afford them, Imogen only need to worry about raising her child and caring for Austin.

Her brother greeted her at the door with a wide smile. The door to the study was ajar, a small room just off the entryway that Imogen used primarily for Dolian's awards. She didn't really have use for an office now that she permanently gave up her blog. Writing about celebrity gossip was just too painful anymore.

Joey was inside, staring at one of Dolian's Oscars that stood on the mantel. He jumped when he heard her, clutching his chest and panting.

"I'm so sorry, Mrs. Crawford!" he murmured.

Imogen frowned at him. Joey had completely changed Austin's quality of life. Hers, too. And it wasn't that she minded having him in the office. Since the day he was hired, she made it clear that she wanted him to feel at home.

"What are you doing in here?" she settled on asking.

He exhaled slowly, rubbing his palms against his hips. Glancing at the awards again, Joey shrugged. "I'm just such a big fan," Joey finally admitted. "Some would even call me his biggest one! That was why I was so excited to come work for you."

Possessively placing a hand on her growing belly, where Dolian's child kicked against her palm, Imogen said simply, "No, dear. You're not."

THE END

ACKNOWLEDGMENTS

Thank you so, so much for sticking with me on another thriller! The concept of obsession and where the dividing line is between obsession and fanaticism has always fascinated me. If you knew me in my teenage years, you know that I toed that line for far too long. I'm glad it all worked out for me in the end. Maybe it will someday for Imogen.

It wouldn't be a Samantha Gail book if I didn't acknowledge my amazing co-workers. Thank you for your continued support of all my bookish endeavors. You have stayed with me through every sleepless night and crazy story, and I can't begin to tell you how much it means to me.

To all of my incredible readers down in the trenches with me as I write in multiple genres and constantly pivot as new ideas take hold, you are the reason I continue to write. You always show up for me and it means the world. Specifically, thank you to my own number one fan, Toni Baker, and all my book club girlies: Janessa, Morgan, Sarah, Chantel, Renee, Ally, Maddie, Felicia, and Heather.

My mom, Kelly, my deepest thanks for becoming a reader simply because you believe in me. Who knew that all I had to do for you to pick up a book is write one? Bonding over my books is one of the greatest blessings to come from this adventure. I'm grateful for you.

I put so many late nights into this book that I should probably acknowledge all the coffee companies who made it possible. Y'all are the real MVP's. Once you figure out a way to just set up an IV drip of caffeine, let me know.

Jack, Tristan, and Cael, we did it again. I love you more than words can say.

-SG

ABOUT THE AUTHOR

Samantha Gail is a former Probation Parole Officer who supervised sex offenders before deciding she needed something with happily ever afters. Her work falls into multiple genres, primarily, thriller, romance, and fantasy. She currently manages a bookstore and writes when she's not spending time with her three children and three fur babies.

Samantha loves to connect with readers and watches her Instagram DM's like a hawk! Don't hesitate to reach out with questions, reviews, or requests!

ALSO BY SAMANTHA GAIL

Pay the Price

Epoch

Full Circle